"You're a coffee shop?" Kevin ventured.

The mug was placed on the counter in front of an empty barstool.

"Coffee's free," the man said. "Conversation, too. Everything else…" he made a slow arcing glance drawing Kevin's attention to the numerous shelves crowded to overflowing with bric-a-brac and sundry, with no particular order to it.

"The 'goods and services.'" Kevin straddled the barstool and took a sip. The coffee was hot but not too hot, strong but not too strong, and had a hint of cinnamon that he could actually taste. Usually flavored coffees smelled great to him but, ultimately, all ended up tasting like bitter coffee in the end.

The man cocked his head toward the plate glass window. The burned out letter O was weakly trying to flicker back to life. "I thought I fixed that sign," he mused. He gently smacked the back of it with his hand. The letter O buzzed in annoyance before settling back into it's previous darkened state.

Kevin smiled despite his mood. "Only Fonzie can fix broken neon with a smack," he said. "Probably just a loose wire."

"To be sure," the man said. "Loosened it myself."

Gods and Services: New Location

Gods & Services: New Location

Edited by R.J. Carter

Critical Blast Publishing
624 Sunnyhill Drive
Belleville, IL 62223

ISBN: 978-1-967199-91-4

DEDICATION

To Cronos, who gives time, takes time, and causes it to slip away.

CONTENTS

ACKNOWLEDGMENTS

This book would not exist without the faith and trust of the contributing writers who rose to the challenge, armed with the greatest weapon ever created: imagination.

THE SHOP...
R. J. Carter

The sky was appropriately overcast as Kevin walked, lost in thought. The service had been nice, or so he was told. He had been assured many times that his mother would have loved it, although Kevin wondered how anybody could love something that ended with them being sealed in a box and buried under six feet of dirt forever.

He walked an aimless path, not ready to go back home to the empty house. In fact, he had no destination in mind at all, he just needed to amble, to be in motion, to think. Hands in pocket, eyes cast down at the sidewalk, he numbly counted cracks as he stepped over them. In the back of his mind, he remembered the macabre childhood rhyme:

step on a crack

break your mother's back.

It wasn't a broken back that had taken her, and it certainly wasn't Kevin's fault. But that didn't serve as a balm for the guilt he carried. The last conversation he'd had with his mother on the phone had been, as usual, an aggravating one. She talked and talked and talked, and always insisted that she knew what was best for Kevin. It didn't matter that most of the time she did, it was still annoying. And this last time, this very last time, Kevin had finally had enough. He snapped at her. He hung up on her. He ignored the ring tone of the immediate callback. And for what? A few hours of not listening to her constant yammering? A brief respite?

He kicked at a rock in his path, sending it skittering down the concrete path.

She'd gotten on the bus shortly after the call. No doubt thinking there was a problem with Kevin's phone service, because surely no decent son would just hang up on his mother and then ignore her calls, right?

Kevin did eventually answer his phone later that afternoon, even though he did not recognize the number. The call where the serious sounding man confirmed his identity, then asked him to come downtown so he could confirm his mother's identity, the identity of the woman in the morgue, pulled from the wreckage of the bus that had drifted into the wrong lane of traffic.

He caught up to the pebble and kicked it again, watched it bounce erratically down the walk. The toe of well-worn brown leather loafer came down on it gently, halting its path. Kevin lifted his eyes and saw the owner of the loafers. He was thin and a little lanky, with gray hair and an ageless face, leaning against the door jamb of a little shop. He could have been forty, he could have been seventy, it was hard to tell. He glanced at Kevin over silver-rimmed spectacles with a wan smile.

"You're looking mighty low, son," the gray man said with soft amiability. "Coming from or going to?"

Kevin blinked. "Excuse me?"

"The funeral," the man said. "Coming from or going to?"

"Coming… Wait, how did you…?"

"Know it was a funeral?" He smiled thinly. "Doesn't take a Sherlock to figure that out. Black suit, hands in pockets, and a thunderstorm about to break. Not likely to be a wedding, although I reckon I've seen a groom or two who might have felt the same."

Kevin glanced up at the sky. The man was right. He hadn't noticed how quickly overcast had turned to ominous. The clouds weren't just dark. They were threatening — black, bubbling cumulonimbus titans. As he looked, nickel-sized blobs of rain began to smack hard against his cheek.

"That's my signal to go back inside," the man said, turning toward the door of the shop behind him. "You're welcome to pop in till it blows over."

The rain was picking up quickly. For a moment, Kevin thought to decline the offer and just make a sprint for the nearest subway station. Whether it was the rain or his mood, he found it difficult to get his bearings. He couldn't make out the landmarks, and the rain had become a wall of water obscuring his vision of the nearest street signs. He quickly pulled up his collar and turned toward the shop. A little neon sign lit up a single plate glass window, declaring the offering of "Goods & Services." Kevin noted one of the letter O's had burned out.

A bell mounted inside above the doorway tinkled as Kevin pushed his way into the shop. The gray man had moved behind a glass counter with an old brass cash register. He was pouring two mugs of coffee from a carafe — one of three full pots that sat side by side in cheap Mr. Coffee machines.

"You're a coffee shop?" Kevin ventured.

The mug was placed on the counter in front of an empty barstool. "Coffee's free," the man said. "Conversation, too. Everything else…" he made a slow arcing glance drawing Kevin's attention to the numerous shelves crowded to overflowing with bric-a-brac and sundry, with no particular order to it.

"The 'goods and services.'" Kevin straddled the barstool and took a sip. The coffee was hot but not too hot, strong but not too strong, and had a hint of cinnamon that he could actually taste. Usually flavored coffees smelled great to him but, ultimately, all ended up tasting like bitter coffee in the end.

The man cocked his head toward the plate glass window. The burned out letter O was weakly trying to flicker back to life. "I thought I fixed that sign," he mused. He gently smacked the back of it with his hand. The letter O buzzed in annoyance before settling back into it's previous darkened state.

Kevin smiled despite his mood. "Only Fonzie can fix broken neon with a smack," he said. "Probably just a loose wire."

"To be sure," the man said. "Loosened it myself."

Kevin crinkled his eyes. "You want the light not to work?"

The older man gave a thin smile and pulled a business card from his shirt pocket. "Sign should match the card," he said as he passed it across the counter. Kevin picked it up and read the plain type face on the plain white cardboard:

GODS & SERVICES

HIRAM PRIEST, PROPRIETOR

He looked up as Hiram took out a handkerchief and polished his spectacles. "No phone number? No email address?"

Hiram registered mild surprise. "Not usually the first thing out of people's mouths," he said. "But I've never really needed either one. Shop always tends to find people when it needs something."

The shop owner had a funny way of talking, Kevin thought. He couldn't decide if the accent was Maine or Mississippi, but his folksy way of putting things reminded him of — well, not his own grandfather, but somebody's grandfather. He took another sip and took in the shelves. Not just shelves, but antique wall hooks, cheap plastic tubs, museum quality urns (reproductions, surely), all jumbled together in a helter-skelter array. Anyone looking for a specific something would be hard pressed to find it quickly.

"Encourages browsing," Hiram said, reading Kevin's thoughts.

Kevin's eyes landed on a headscarf. It was long and colorful and had seen better days although Kevin thought it might brighten up a bit with a gentle washing.

"Mom would love that," he said, mostly to himself.

"Your mother a runner?" Hiram asked.

"No," Kevin said. "No, she isn't. Wasn't. Sorry. She died."

"Sorry to hear that." Hiram lifted the scarf from the knob over which it was draped. He laid it lengthwise across the counter. "Reckon that was the funeral in question."

Kevin nodded numbly, then caught himself. "Why'd you ask if she was a runner?"

"Because of your interest in the scarf, naturally," Hiram replied as though it should have been obvious. His long fingers stroked the length of the scarf, smoothing out the wrinkles and creating furrows. "It isn't your typical woman's accessory."

HEADSCARVES AND HEADWINDS

Robert Allen Lupton

I woke up before sunrise Saturday morning and dressed in four hundred dollars' worth of color-coordinated running gear. I looked in the full-length mirror and adjusted my purple and gold headband. The gold matched my shorts and socks. The purple was the same color as my top and my shoes cost more than my prom dress.

My running belt held four small water bottles. I put on mirrored sunglasses, clipped my phone to the belt, and put on my earbuds. "Sharp Dressed Man" played as I ran out the door.

I dashed down the driveway, crossed the street, and ran up the hill toward the park. I waved hello to a retired couple walking their Pomeranian and concentrated on maintaining my stride mechanics as I jogged up the incline.

Two blocks later I entered the park, ran to a sitting area, braced myself on a trash can near the benches, and threw up. My legs quivered, throbbed, and gave way while I fought to hold myself upright. I clutched the filth-incrusted garbage can like a drunk hugging a lamppost.

When the nausea passed, I limped three steps and plopped my 225-pound body onto a rusty metal bench. I rinsed my mouth with a water bottle and cursed my doctor.

What the hell was Doctor Carson thinking with all that 'running is good for you' crap?

My annual physical was a month ago. Dr. Alice Carson took my vitals, reviewed the blood test results, and said, "I don't understand why you aren't dead. You have high blood pressure, and your resting heart rate would be fine if you were a hummingbird. Your body mass index is damn near fifty. It should be twenty-five or less. You have high cholesterol, high glucose, and a worse waist-to-height ratio than Santa Claus.”

“I get it. I’m a little overweight.”

“No, Anna, you’re a lot overweight and a prime candidate for a heart attack or stroke. I can only do so much with medicine. You have to help yourself.”

I hated every inch and pound of her skinny little body. “What the hell am I supposed to do?”

“There’s no magic bullet. Diet and exercise are the only things that work.”

“Do you recommend Waist Watchers or some other diet program?”

“Hell no, they’re all crap and the only weight you’ll lose is from your bank account. You don’t need them, it’s really simple. It’s not easy, but it’s simple. Calories are calories, it doesn’t matter whether a calorie comes from bacon, cookies, or freshly caught salmon. If you use more calories than you eat, you lose weight. If you don’t, you gain weight. It’s not magic.”

“How do I know how much I can eat and how much to exercise? Is there a chart or something?”

“Pick a target weight, I suggest 140 pounds. That’s eighty-five pounds less than you weigh now, but you can lose that much in a year. Your body needs ten calories a day to support each pound of body weight. If you eat two thousand calories, then you need to burn, or exercise away, six hundred calories a day. Write down your calorie intake and your daily exercise. Trust me, keeping a log makes a big difference.”

“What’s the best exercise?”

“Running burns more calories per minute than anything else, but don’t try to run tomorrow, you’ll have to work up to it. Walk every day for a few weeks before you try to run. Eighty-five pounds a year is less than two pounds per week. You don’t want to lose weight any faster than that.”

“Crap, in a year I’ll be thirty-five years old.”

“You’ll be thirty-five years old next year whether you lose the weight or not, assuming you live that long.”

Doctor Carson gave me the contact information for

three women's training programs. "Everyone needs a support group."

I met with the groups, picked one, and they assigned Donna as my sponsor. It was like AA. I bought running gear and started walking every morning. I lost four pounds in two weeks.

That morning I'd planned to run a mile. Instead, I ended up on a park bench and half crippled with dry heaves. I love this shit.

"Good morning," someone said and I turned to look. An old man was sweeping the entrance to a second-hand store. What was a store doing in the middle of the park? The neon sign flashed erratically on and off. One of the Os in the word 'Goods" was burned out and the sign read 'Gods and Services.'

The old man smiled. "Just opening up. Come on in. You never know what you'll find."

"My knee hurts. Do you have anything to help with that?"

"You never know."

I went inside. The store smelled like used gym clothes that had fermented in a locker for a week. Everything inside was jumbled together. The old man said, "Name's Priest, Hiram Priest. I've got what you need right here."

He handed me a dirty strip of linen. It had once been golden colored, but it had faded to a pale yellow that reminded me of a baby's diaper. "Seriously?"

"Bought it at a garage sale. I think it used to be a headband or headscarf, but you can wrap your knee with it."

"It's filthy and it smells old enough to have belonged to a gladiator."

"Yes, dear, it does. Sometimes old things are special. Wrap your knee. It's only a dollar."

"Don't have any money with me."

"I like those red, white, and blue wristbands. Trade you."

I made the trade, wrapped my knee, and walked out into the park. I heard a whoosh behind me. The shop, flickering neon sign and all, was gone.

My knee still hurt and I'd probably get an infection from the filthy headband or whatever it was.

I silently begged God to kill me quickly. "Please don't make me do this for six months and then kill me. Please, take me now." God didn't answer.

I wiped my forehead on my sleeve and decided silent prayer was overrated. "God or Goddess, angel or demon, or anyone else up there, either give me strength or kill me now."

The sprinklers in the park came on and I limped quickly out of the line of fire. I was soaked from the waist down. "Nice. Hell of an answer, God," I screamed.

"You don't have to shout; I can hear you."

My knee hurt too much to jump, but I flinched and dropped a water bottle. I looked around and didn't see anyone. "This isn't funny, who's there?"

"Down here."

I looked down and there was a small perfectly formed woman wearing a tightly cinched chiton, a traditional Greek dress, and laced leather sandals. Her black hair was tied in a ponytail. "Great," I said. "Crippled, sick, and I'm having hallucinations. I ask God for help and he sends a dress-up doll."

I didn't know that running would deprive my brain of oxygen. I'd read about the runner's high, but I didn't think it worked like that. I figured that once I'd started hallucinating, I might as well play along and I asked, "Did you bring Ken with you?"

"I don't know a Ken. Is he from Sparta?"

"Never mind. What the hell are you?"

"You prayed to either die or to run better. I heard you and I'm here to help."

"I prayed to God, not to a Barbie doll."

"I am a god. I'm Atalanta, the goddess of runners."

Other people were walking into the park, and I didn't want them to see the crazy lady with vomit on her shirt talking to a little girl's toy. "You're not even a foot tall, I thought a god would be bigger."

Atalanta noticed my furtive glances at the other people and said, "Don't worry, nobody else can see or hear me. However, they can hear you. If that bothers you, we should go somewhere more private."

I stood and said, "Yeah, let's get the psycho lady out of the park." My left leg buckled on the first step and I sat back on the bench.

The woman took my calf in her small hands, unwrapped my knee, and said, "Relax, I can help. This is a headscarf, you know. Don't ever wash it and wear it whenever you run." The warmth from her fingers spread through my legs like a sip of warm brandy on a cold night. I could feel my muscles loosen and strengthen as waves of power spread from ankle to hip. After a moment, she put her hands on my other leg with the same result.

My legs were stronger, but I was still nauseated and dizzy. I took three quick steps and thought I was going to pass out. The park played spin the bottle.

Atalanta put her hand on my ankle and the merry-go-round stopped. She said, "I've shared some of my power and strength with you, but it won't last long. We should go?"

It was easy for her to keep up with me and ten minutes later she climbed onto my dinette table. I sat on a red vinyl-covered chair and looked the little goddess in the eye. "Amazing, you're still here. Tell me again, who are you?"

"I'm Atalanta, the goddess of runners. My small size is a reflection of how few people still worship me. Almost no one remembers me and a forgotten goddess is a small goddess."

"I've never heard of you."

"Of course, you haven't. I never had a temple, but every running track and racecourse is sacred to me. I receive a small portion of power whenever people gather and run. Whenever two rivals sprint toward a finish line, their efforts strengthen me. These small and unacknowledged dribbles of worship have kept me alive. Small, but alive."

"How can you help me?"

"We're going to help each other. I will help you grow strong, lose weight, and run properly. Your form is terrible.

You will honor me, pray to me, and spread my worship to other runners. As your strength grows, so will my own. When I gain power, you'll gain power. It's your decision. If you want my help, pray to me before you run. You need to speak loudly and ask for my help." She smiled and walked behind the box of Cocoa Puffs I'd left on the table.

I picked up the box and she wasn't there. The hallucination was fun while it lasted. I ate two bowls of ice cream with chocolate sprinkles to celebrate my five-minute run.

I looked up Atalanta on the internet. She was the daughter of King Iasus. He'd wanted a son and left her on a mountaintop to die. She was raised by a female bear and grew up strong, fast, and tough enough to spit nails. After a series of adventures, she was reunited with her father. He tried to marry her off, but she didn't want to be anyone's wife. She was faster and stronger than any man she'd ever met and had decided to remain a virgin.

She finally agreed that she'd marry the first man who could beat her in a footrace. However, any man who raced her and lost would be put to death. A lot of men tried and failed. She met Hippomenes and fell in love, but she wasn't willing to throw a race. Hippomenes prayed to Aphrodite for help.

Aphrodite gave him three golden apples to carry during the race. Whenever he threw one of the apples on the ground, Atalanta stopped to pick it up. The strategy worked and Hippomenes won.

The legend says the young couple celebrated by making love in Aphrodite's temple. Aphrodite was appalled by this lack of respect and turned them both into lions. I didn't think being turned into a lion was all that bad, she could have turned them into pigs.

It couldn't hurt, so I decided I'd pray to Atalanta before I ran. The next morning, I put on my running gear, headscarf and all, locked the front door behind me, checked to make sure there was no one around, and said, "Great Atalanta, mighty goddess of the run, grant me strength and stamina this morning. Today, I run in your honor." I tried really hard to sell it, in for a penny, in for a pound.

There was no puff of smoke or flash of light, but Atalanta appeared instantly. She was dressed in Nike running clothes from head to foot. I looked questioningly at her outfit, and she said, "I liked Nike, she was always nice to me."

She reached up and said, "I'll run with you. Remember, no one else can see me. Bend down and touch my hands."

I felt the warmth spread through my body. After a moment, she released my hands and we ran down the street. We ran three miles in thirty-eight minutes, amazingly fast by my standards.

We ran together every morning and I lost three more pounds in the first week. I asked how long this was going to take and she said, "It's not magic. Two or three pounds a week is enough. You'll get stronger and faster with every run. In about six months, I'll want you to race other people."

"Six months, can't you just do your goddess thing and make me thin and fast right now?"

"I said it doesn't work like that. Everything has a price, there's no such thing as free wine. You have to stomp your own grapes. The gods help those who help themselves."

Saturday mornings, I ran with my sponsor, Donna, and the training group. I kept my word to Atalanta and prayed to her before I ran. I prayed for her to give strength and stamina to all the runners. The other women teased me about it for the first few weeks.

The other women stopped teasing me after I'd lost twenty-five pounds and could run them into the ground. Donna was the first to join me in prayer. She said, "I've been a Methodist, a Wiccan, and a Libertarian, but none of that crap worked. I'll pray to an ancient Greek goddess, what's the worst that could happen?" Before long a dozen of us formed a prayer circle every Saturday morning and prayed to Atalanta.

I was the only one who could see her. I grew thinner and faster and she grew taller. She said, "Only Donna and two of the other women pray to me every time they run. It'll help if the other women pray more than once a week. I need them to pray every day. The stronger I am, the stronger I can make you."

On Labor Day weekend, Donna and I ran six miles in sixty-two minutes. I weighed less than 190 pounds. Donna's fiancée, Martin, ran with us that morning. Technically, he didn't run with us, he raced us.

Martin said, "Let's make this a little more exciting. Loser buys breakfast." He took off before I finished double-knotting my shoelaces. Donna left right behind him. I said, "Atalanta, help me." He was fifty yards ahead of me when I started.

My little goddess ran right beside me. "Don't try to catch the bastard all at once. You only have to be five seconds a mile faster than him. He's a jackass and will go out too fast. Trust me, he'll fall apart. Stay with me. You can do this."

Like I said, I ran six miles in sixty-two minutes. Martin got as much as a quarter mile ahead of me, but he went to pieces before he'd run five miles. I blew right by him and had time to change my shirt before he finished. Atalanta said, "That's my girl."

My celebration was cut short at breakfast. Martin got a piece of bacon caught in his throat and choked to death. Donna and the manager both tried the Heimlich maneuver, but couldn't dislodge the bacon. He died on the greasy restaurant floor.

I didn't run for a week. I stayed with Donna through the funeral and helped her clean Martin's stuff out of her place. By the next Saturday, my body was screaming for exercise. It hurt me more to not run than it used to hurt when I ran.

That morning, Donna and I met the girls in our running group, they all hugged Donna and we had a nice group cry. We prayed to Atalanta and started a five-mile loop run. Atalanta ran by my side. She was two feet tall, twice the size she was when I first met her.

Even though I'd taken a week off, I felt great. Atalanta said, "I'm more powerful today and because I'm more powerful, I can make you stronger. We help each other. Don't take a week off again, it's not good for either of us."

I told her Martin had choked to death and Atalanta said, "He was a pig. Choking on bacon is what he deserved. Forget about him. Don't let anything stop your training. We get weaker if you don't run."

I didn't take a day off for two weeks and my weight dropped to 180 pounds. On the next weekend, Donna and I were the only two in our group who showed up. We held hands and prayed. I could feel the power radiate through me when Atalanta put her hands on my waist.

After the first mile, Donna complained of pain in her right knee. We stopped and she rubbed her leg. "I should've replaced these damn shoes. My knee hurts like hell. Go ahead and run, I'll walk back to the parking lot."

I caught Atalanta's attention and flicked my eyes toward Donna's knee. She shook her head and said in the voice only I could hear. "Only you. I can help the others a little, but I only have enough strength to heal you."

I overtook a man on the trail about a mile after I left Donna. I said good morning between breaths and ran past him. He speeded up and passed me back without saying anything. He slowed down after a few minutes and I ran past him again. He grunted, matched my pace for a couple of hundred yards, and then raced ahead of me.

I caught him again and said, "Let's run together."

He answered by surging to the lead. We seesawed back and forth a few times, but eventually, I pulled away. He ran full speed and tried to catch me in the last quarter mile. His attitude pissed me off, so I sprinted to where Donna was sitting. He didn't catch me.

He took car keys from his running pouch and popped the tailgate on his SUV. He bent over, braced his hands on his knees, and labored to catch his breath. While he was recovering, another car backed across the parking lot and pinned him against his bumper. He was dead before he crumpled to the pavement.

Monday morning, I weighed 170 pounds, and Atalanta was three feet tall. My stomach and legs were taut and firm. I ran an out-and-back that morning, three miles out and three miles back, six miles in fifty-eight minutes. That's faster than ten-minute miles. I couldn't believe it.

I literally worked my butt off for the next two months. After six months of training with Atalanta, I'd dropped seventy-five pounds. Men turned their heads when I ran by. I replaced my entire wardrobe, including my running clothes, even my shoes were a half size smaller. I didn't replace the headband.

I ran twice a day, six days a week. I could run five kilometers in less than twenty-two minutes, that's damn near seven-minute miles. I registered for the Ghosts and Goblins 5K scheduled on Halloween. The week before the race, I had an appointment with Dr. Carson.

"My god, woman, you've lost nearly eighty pounds. No one does that. I tell patients they need to lose weight, and they look guilty and nod their heads in agreement. They go straight home and have a six-pack of beer or pint of ice cream to make themselves feel better. I'm proud of you. Your BMI is still a little high, but it's almost there. The rest of your vital signs are excellent. How did you do this?"

I knew better than to tell her about Atalanta. Doctors aren't inclined to accept divine intervention as a possibility. The old joke goes, "Do you know the difference between God and a doctor?" The answer is "God doesn't think he's a doctor." I gave Dr. Carson all the credit. I explained how hard I'd worked to follow her advice. I talked about the joys of sunrise runs and my support group. I was enthusiastic when I discussed rain gear and running in the snow. I never mentioned prayer or headbands.

Dr. Carson was impressed and asked if I would be willing to mentor a few of her more physically challenged patients.

"I've been planning to start my own running support group. If I could help six or seven other women, I'd be thrilled. I feel like a cancer survivor who feels obligated to help other women who have the same issues I had, but I don't want any men in my group."

"Is there a reason you don't want to mentor any men?"

"I haven't been in a relationship since I was thirty. Hank and I lived together for six years after graduate school. We'd scheduled our wedding. I worked sixty hours a week editing textbooks to pay tuition for his doctorate program. Editing is a solitary and sedentary profession. Hank complained that I worked too much."

"Besides," I continued. "Sixty hours a week in front of a computer with a cola on one side and a bag of chips on the other doesn't help your waistline. Hank met a cute little steel-bellied piece of fluff sunning herself by the community pool and the bastard was gone."

"Didn't you try to meet anyone else?"

'Nope, I spent eighty hours a week on the computer. Cola mixed with vodka really kicks up the calorie count and cookies are better than chips. I managed to gain twenty pounds a year until you bitch-slapped me back into reality. The weight was a lot more fun to gain than it's been to lose."

"I'm sorry I asked you about men. May I have some of my female patients call you?"

"Let me call them. Send me their contact information."

Donna and the rest of my running group met me thirty minutes before the Ghost and Goblin 5K was scheduled to start. We held hands, prayed to Atalanta, loosened up, and headed to the starting line. This was a local fun run with no elite runners. Six hundred men, women, and children lined up on the school playground which served as the starting and finishing line.

I ran the 5K in nineteen minutes, faster than seven minutes a mile. I beat all of the women and most of the men. A man came up to me after the race, introduced himself, and asked me out.

I couldn't speak for a minute. I told him no and he turned away. A five-foot-tall Atalanta shoved me and said, "His name is Ray, tell him yes. Meet him for a run and breakfast. You can't hide from men for the rest of your life. It'll be good for both of us."

I caught him and we planned to meet for a run and breakfast the next Sunday. During the week, I ran twice every day, contacted Dr. Carson's patients, and scheduled a group meeting with them for Saturday morning.

When I met with the women, I told them my story. A good success story motivates people. I included the legend of Atalanta and said that I pray to her before I run because it helps me focus. I don't know if the women took me seriously or not, but some of them looked uncomfortable

Katrina, one of my new recruits, said, "Honey, I've tried everything else. I'd pray to the devil himself if he'd help with these thighs. It can't hurt. Let's do it."

I coached the group through warm-up exercises, stretches, and prayer. All six women ran two miles that morning and they were overjoyed. After the run, I handed out a printed running schedule for the next three weeks and a copy of a prayer they could use. I told them to meet me next Saturday. Same time, same place, faster pace.

Katrina asked me, "You wear your headscarf tied so that the long ends are flapping behind you when you run into a headwind. Doesn't that make you crazy?"

"No, it doesn't. It makes me feel fast. If you run fast enough, you're always running into a headwind."

I hardly slept that night. Meeting Ray, my prospective running buddy, for breakfast and a run was my first date in six years. The run was great, and he was charming at breakfast. I agreed to meet him again the next Sunday.

Life was pretty damn good for the next month. I loved mentoring the girls and Atalanta grew taller. I ran six-minute miles every day and Sunday mornings with Ray were wonderful. After our third run together, I took him home for breakfast. He stayed for a little more exercise, a shower, and lunch.

When we ran, Ray used his cell phone to track his mileage. He wore it in a carrier on his right bicep. The carrier had a clear plastic cover so Ray could see the screen and monitor his distance, pace, and time. He kept the phone in silent mode. We were five miles into our fifth run together when his phone lit up. I was running right next to him and saw the screen filled with a photo of a blonde and two kids. The phone identified the caller as "home". Three pairs of blue eyes stared at me.

"You son of a bitch! You're married." I pushed him into the bushes and sprinted down the trail. He got to his feet and hurried after me.

I didn't look back. The sounds of his footsteps faded every minute. He begged me to wait. He screamed the customary protestations of innocence and swore he could explain. I never turned my head, and I beat him to the parking lot by a quarter mile.

I was changing shoes when he walked up. I threw a water bottle at him and missed. It's hard to aim through tears. He held his hands out in supplication, took two more steps toward me, and collapsed on the pavement.

The EMT said it was an aneurysm. Ray had died instantly.

I prayed to Atalanta when I got home. She appeared in a designer bikini and expensive sunglasses. She was taller than me now, over six feet.

I recounted the three men who'd died after running with me and she said, "I know. They were asses and deserved to die. That's why I took them."

"Took them?"

"I'm a goddess. My strength is dependent on worship and sacrifice. The more worshipers I have, the more power I have. The more power I have, the better for both of us. You remember my legend. If a man races me and loses, he dies. You're my human avatar. Any man who races you and loses is mine. Nothing provides power to a god better than human sacrifice. It's one hell of a rush."

"I didn't know."

"Don't lie to yourself, Anna. Did you think I helped you because you have cute dimples? I told you from the start - we help each other."

"I beat a couple of hundred men when I ran the Ghost and Goblin 5K and none of them died."

"For a man to become a sacrifice, he has to actually try to beat you. The men who ran in the goblin race didn't run against you; they ran with you. There wasn't a man in that race that cared whether he beat you or not. They cared about finishing and they cared about how fast they ran.

They didn't give a damn about you. The three men who've died wanted to beat you. They punched their own tickets in the sacrifice lottery."

"I didn't know. I didn't agree to this."

"You never asked. I told you nothing is free. Everything has a price. You didn't complain when you weighed less every week. I don't recall any remorse when you checked how much faster you ran. You're acting like someone who wants the bacon but can't stand to kill the pig. Grow up."

"I quit. I won't do this anymore."

"If that's what you want, fine, but you can be a world-class runner in a year. You're almost fast enough already. Or, if you like, I'll return the pounds and the knee pain. It's up to you. It's not like we're hurting men who don't ask for it."

"I don't care."

"Yes, you do. I'm a goddess and I know when you don't tell the truth. Don't lie to me and don't lie to yourself. I could coddle you this afternoon until you admit what you want, but I don't have the time or the patience. I have a pedicure in Rio in an hour. Stop protesting and register for more races. I need more sacrifices. Next time you race, shove some man, bump him, curse him, or step on his feet. Make him angry. Make him want to beat you. I'll be discrete and wait a couple of days before I harvest him."

"I don't know, I'll have to think about it."

Atalanta said, "You do that, sweetheart. I'm off to Rio. I'll see you and the girls on Saturday."

I'm a terrible person. I remember weighing over 225 pounds and holding my breath to tie my shoes. I used to gasp for breath after I walked across a room. I reminded myself how well my relationships had turned out and I said to myself, "Piss on them all, they're assholes."

I went online and registered for a Thanksgiving Day race, the Turkey Trot.

I deliberately ran slower than usual for the first mile of the Turkey Trot. I picked out a couple of likely-looking men. Former jocks who still think they're God's gift to women have a special arrogance that shines like sunrise. I picked one and ran behind him. I stepped on his heel and made him stumble.

I grabbed him to keep him from falling and said, "If you're too hungover or clumsy to run, get off the trail."

He jerked his arm away from me and sped up. I let him run ahead for a couple of minutes and then caught him. I stepped on his foot again, laughed, and ran past him.

He staggered for a few steps, regained his balance, and shouted at me, "You bitch, you did that on purpose."

I sneered and said, "Grow a pair, don't be a crybaby."

He chased me all the way to the finish line. I checked my time, twenty-two minutes, and disappeared into the crowd before he could find me.

I antagonized three men until they chased me during the Jingle Bell Run and one on New Year's morning at the Auld Lang Syne Five Miler. I ran the Valentine's Day Run for Love 10K in forty minutes and had five angry men chasing me when I finished. I could have run it faster, but the men needed to feel like they had a chance.

During my morning runs, I consistently ran six miles in thirty-three minutes, almost world-class pace. On most days, I felt strong enough to run forever. My weight was down to 120 pounds, and when I looked in the mirror I saw one of those skinny women I used to hate. I love this shit.

Atalanta visited every week. She was seven feet tall and looked better than a runway model. Two days after the Saint Patrick's Leprechaun Run, she woke me in the middle of the night.

"Anna, you were magnificent on Sunday. Four men chased you and all four men lost. I was surprised by how much calling a man a sissy boy pisses him off. I haven't been this tall for two thousand years."

I sat up in bed and said, "I feel stronger than I've ever been. I'm so fast. I want to compete at the Olympic Trials next year. Thank you, I'm sorry I ever complained."

"Don't thank me and don't be sorry," Atalanta said. Her face darkened as if the shadow of hell had eclipsed the sun. She held me down on the bed. "You were right to be worried.

I'm the one who should be sorry. Things never work out well for mortals once they catch the attention of a god."

I didn't know if she was making a pass or getting ready to choke me with a pillow. I struggled and tried to push away her hands, but she was a goddess. "Let me up, you're frightening me."

"I imagine I am," she said and held me so I couldn't move. I broke out in a cold sweat, but I couldn't budge her hands. I wore myself out trying to get away and she didn't even have a hair out of place.

"Why are you doing this? Have you found another avatar? I know I was weak before, but I'm on your side. I want this more than you do."

"The sacrifice of the men after the Celtic road race last weekend gave me the power to take our relationship to the final level. I appreciate everything you've done, but it's time for you to make a sacrifice."

"I've been sacrificing for you since the day we met."

Anger and fire flashed in her eyes. She held both of my arms with one strong hand and grabbed my thigh with the other. "I shared my powers with you. I strengthened these leg muscles, kept them free of injury, and made them limber and supple. I picked you up when you fell, motivated you, and held your hand when you needed consolation. I made sacrifices, not you."

"I sacrificed for you, too. I convinced other women to pray to you. I ran in the heat, the cold, and the rain. You have acolytes for the first time since before Rome ruled the world. I've been loyal."

Her mouth widened in an evil smile and her perfect teeth reflected the moonlight streaming through the window. "Anna, be honest with yourself. You didn't do anything for me. You did those things for yourself. Both you and I are selfish and mean-spirited. Everything we did, we did for ourselves. It's been a fair bargain."

Those bright teeth came closer and I screamed, "You're not going to bite me, are you?"

"Don't be stupid, I'm not a vampire, but I'm tired of being a goddess. One week I'm ten feet tall and the next day I'm the size of a doll. One year, I have altars, priestesses, and worshipers. The next year, I'm hiding from hungry rats in the rubble. When times were really bad, I had to fight pigeons for food. I've been big more times than I can count, but it never lasts. I hate small. It's good to be big and I'm going to quit while I'm big."

She began to glow, and a yellow and orange nimbus enveloped her body. The warm glow spread from her fingers and flowed up my arms and legs. I could feel it sinking beneath my skin. Her breath was visible and it spilled into my mouth and throat. Her glow grew brighter until I couldn't look at her anymore and I closed my eyes. My head swam and I was nauseated for the first time since that morning in the park.

After a moment, I felt the warmth leave my body. The red brightness faded from the inside of my eyelids and my queasiness passed. I opened my eyes and saw myself on the bed. Everything was so big. It took six steps to walk across my bed. I looked down at myself and gasped. I was six inches tall. I looked in the mirror and Atalanta's little face looked back at me.

Atalanta was in my body. Damn. The bitch smiled with my face, picked up my purse, and turned toward me. "I could have harvested you earlier, but I waited until your body was a worthy receptacle. If I were you, I'd stay in the house for a few weeks, it's not safe outside when you're only six inches tall. Cats play pretty rough. If the girls keep praying, you'll grow a foot in the first month. You're tougher than you think and you'll make a great goddess."

Atalanta lied. It took over two months before I gained enough size and strength to leave the house.

***

The first Sunday in June, I saw a woman in new running clothes circling the track at the local high school. She jogged in the predawn darkness because she didn't want anyone to see her. She staggered off the track, limped to the stands, and sat down. She held her head in her hands and tried not to pass out.

The shop, Gods and Services, appeared in the middle of the track. Hiram swept the entrance and called to the woman. A few minutes later, she came out carrying my headband.

She sat down and rubbed her knee. She wrapped it with the headband and muttered, "How the hell does someone twist their knee on a flat running track. This is bullshit. God, you hear me? It's not fair. How about a little help here? God, are you listening to me?"

I knew her name was Sandra, goddesses know these things.

"Good morning, Sandra. I bet your knee really hurts. If you ask me nicely, I can fix it."

***

Kevin stared vacantly, caught up in the older man's yarn despite himself. "So, this Atlanta…"

"Atalanta," Hiram interjected. "Names are vitally important in this business."

"Atalanta," Kevin repeated. "She would have just taken over the running world? Killed a bunch of competitors? Pretty dark ending for a ghost story."

"For a while," Hiram said, flatly. "Nobody really noticed it. Of course, things didn't pan out the way she planned, otherwise I wouldn't have the scarf in stock, would I?"

It dawned on Kevin that the kindly old man actually believed his own story. He turned his head to the store entrance and saw it was still coming down in buckets outside. He weighed the consequences of getting soaked in a strange part of town against staying dry with a possibly crazy person. But then, maybe the guy just liked telling stories. Some people were like that, weren't they? Didn't mean they were dangerous, right? Nevertheless, Kevin nervously stepped back from the loquacious shopkeeper.

"Watch your tuchus," Hiram said benignly. Kevin turned and saw he had nearly backed into the tip of an arrow — a concrete arrow held in a shooting position by a concrete cherub.

"What the heck," he exclaimed. "Shouldn't you tape some foam or something around that? Someone could get hurt."

Hiram shrugged. "Most customers walk forward when they shop around," he said. "Helps them to see what's looking for them."

An older model flip phone began skittering across the counter as an incoming call set it vibrating. Hiram made no move to answer it, looking almost lost in thought at the stone effigy with the bow and arrow. "Funny thing about those statues. Everyone always associates Cupid with the thrill of new love. But that's not always the way of these things."

THE BARN CUPID

Lawrence Dagstine

Oscar Heartdale belonged to a Protestant community that expected every man and woman to perform the duties of several persons simultaneously and with perfection, often mixed with an atmosphere of breathless haste. He wasn't a firm believer in technology. He wasn't the biggest fan of automation. Instead, he welcomed the opportunity to relax and measure his life, face its inadequacies, fan the divine spark within him rather than glue his eyeballs to some piece of tech so that he might more clearly approximate the person he wished to be.

When his wife, Danitha, was alive, they had had their cozy silence by the living room fire in winter, while the dogs lay on the hearthrug. In summer they sat on the back porch in the old glider, holding hands. Sharing the silence in love made it a joy. But today he was restless, incapable of detaching himself from the thought of all he had to do. He was also incapable of letting go of that feeling of emptiness and loneliness, melancholic matters the old Quaker population used to refer to as "creaturely activity," a time to center down.

The orchard was getting beyond him; everything ripened at once. Beyond the glade and the lush, rich pastures, it was a rare morning, probably just as rare a scenery; there might not be a day so beautiful till next summer. Oscar started for the barn to get ready for shocking corn. But as he stepped out of the warm sunshine into the chilly interior, it came over him like a God-given leading that it was not a sin to celebrate this superb day.

He walked to the back of the barn where there were several haystacks, a wheelbarrow, a pitchfork leaning upright, a rusted buoy, an old seaman's bell in desperate need of a polish, and a statue covered by a plaster-stained drop cloth.

Oscar pulled the cloth away. The sunlight from the hole in the barn's archway shone fervently down on that spot. The statue was representative of a teenage cherub with male and female anatomy, aiming a bow and arrow fiercely at the sky. The white and grayscale sculpture was more realistic than anything the local museums could offer, a lifelike idol fashioned in accordance with Greek myth and chiseled to absolute perfection. The way it was shaped was no easy task, cut in a durable mix of plaster, marble, and granite, smoothed out in just the right places, with a wide circular base. Matter of fact, it was the most exquisite statue he had ever laid his eyes upon. Danitha had commissioned it six months before her death. After her burial it was completed. The artist refused compensation, quickly disappearing from the community, never to be heard from again.

There were small stone figures sticking out of the base's marble, two of the figures a couple standing hand in hand, evidently posing in a way to be "loving and faithful, so long as they both shall live." Both wore masterfully carved expressions of elation. There was no figure of a minister. There was, however, a small church fashioned out of clay. This ornamentation seemed rushed. Other figures sat behind the couple on plaster-made benches. Most of the male figures wore broad-brimmed hats. All the women figures had long dresses and bonnets. The cherub's left leg was raised high above their heads, back arched, body tilted.

"No. Don't you go creating any miracles for me," Oscar said, looking up at the decorative laurel positioned firmly atop the statue's head. "You can fire that thing all you want," he said of the bow and arrow. "I'll never fall in love again. I refuse to."

He lost track of time, not knowing how long he exchanged words with the cherub, not realizing how long he clutched the damning memory of Danitha to him. But he finally threw the drop cloth back over the statue, ran out of the barn, reached the edge of the glade and saw the granite stone of Danitha's grave.

"Not today," he muttered. "Today we embark on the unheard of."

So he did an unheard-of thing. He turned on his heel, walked toward the estuary, exited the glade, and headed for Tranquility Pond. The larger than average body of water was private, shared between eight different properties and their owners' thirst for sailing. He, who was so conscientious, who cared for his land as if it were part of his soul—he, Oscar Heartdale, ran away to sea!

Sort of.

The dogs quickly sniffed his trail and came running after him. He could tell the Labrador mixes were ecstatic. Young Lottie, the retriever, loped ahead on her long legs; poor, affectionate little Dodo, the ailing twelve-year-old yellow and black German coated, could barely keep up with the estuary path. By the time they reached the pond, Lottie was already in the dory, but Dodo hesitated, looking over the edge of the dock. Usually she jumped bravely, too. Now she stood there, anguished, lurching forward tentatively, then pulling back in fear. Oscar tucked her tightly under his arm as he stepped into the small boat, not quite so resilient himself as in his early days, but ably enough. Untying the painter, he cast off, rowing slowly, disregarding the statue and leaving his cares ashore.

The pond was still, but Oscar could hear the surf crashing beyond the estuary dunes. Exhilarated by the clear air, gliding over the glassy water, he felt as soul-satisfied as the dogs now appeared to be, curled up in the stern. Drifting lazily, he gave himself up to the delight of reliving the maritime events of recent weeks—boating was his greatest escape—which was something that always took his mind off Danitha.

# # #

One day in August, Sally Streisand, the community director from Township Hall, had brought over an unexpected guest. Oscar had been on the living room floor, playing with her son Mathew, when an attractive woman walked into the living room. The soft creases in her face, deepening as she smiled, made no illusion of her age. Neither did the white hair, cut short and simply combed. She moved easily, her arms and legs soft but fragile looking, and her open, unaffected manner gave the impression that she was younger than her years. Yet, at the same time, there was this impeccable but mysterious air about her.

"Sorry I'm late," Sally said. "Hope the babysitting wasn't a pain."

"Not at all," Oscar said, looking down at Mathew. "Matty and I were just building the most impregnable fortress with these here Lego. Weren't we, Matty?"

"Hey Matty! Mommy's back!" The toddler, who couldn't have been older than three, jumped into his mother's arms and gave her a tight hug. "I didn't think I would be outside this long. I can't thank you enough." She looked to her female companion. "Oh, I hope you don't mind that I brought a guest."

"Of course not." Oscar struggled to sit up, his jerky elderly movements causing the Legos to collapse with a crash, scattering the blocks across the room. He felt like a fool. "There goes our fortress."

Mathew was hilarious. "He busted it!" he shouted gleefully. He dropped an armful of Lego figurines on the ruins and ran back to his mother.

"Matty, I want you to put all these blocks back in their bucket."

"Yes, Mommy."

Sally was bending over Oscar now, holding out a helping hand, talking all the while. "Oscar, this is Ms. Adrestia. I happened to be in Township Hall when she walked into our hall of records. I overheard her tell the cataloguer that her ancestors were local Quakers, and she wanted to find out about them." Mathew was tugging at Sally's skirt, begging to be noticed. She placed her free hand on his head lovingly as she went on. "No one knows as much about Quakers as she does, Oscar. So I asked Ms. Adrestia to come home with me for supper."

Sally bent to kiss Mathew. Then, turning back to her guest, she asked, "By the way, what's your first name?"

"Eros." It was enunciated slowly, distinctly, as if the owner were accustomed to having her name misheard.

Oscar caught his breath. "Eros," he muttered aloud, having heard it before. "He, rather than she, known as the Roman counterpart of Cupid."

"They are one and the same, I can assure you," the woman said. "I was a historian and museum curator for half my life. Both are the forerunner to the cherubic Renaissance child of love, the embodiment of sexual prowess."

Oscar was impressed. "I'm not one for love stories these days, but mythology tells of a romance between Eros and a woman named Psyche. Aphrodite was extremely jealous of Psyche, an envy based upon beauty and mortality. They say men were leaving alters barren just to worship this mere human."

"You know your stuff." Now the woman was impressed. "But some would go as far as to say Eros and Psyche were of the same mold, as one, the son and daughter of Aphrodite, only in a constant celestial cycle of love and companionship. Both inseparable, both intertwined, they were souls who shared the same anatomy and whose interventions in the love affairs of gods and mortals caused magic bonds of the purest love to develop, often illicitly."

"And your last name. Adrestia," Oscar murmured under his tongue, enchanted. Where had he heard it before? It eluded him. "An ancient name, isn't it?" he guessed.

"It stands for girl who cannot escape." The woman's face lit up. "You know, you're the first person I ever met who knows their stuff. Most people think, because they've never heard it, that it's a joke, corny. It's been a trial all my life. I nearly changed it."

"I think it's beautiful," Oscar assured her. "It goes quite well with Eros."

"I know how confusing introductions can be when your name isn't common," Eros exclaimed.

Oscar finally shook the woman's outstretched hand. He was glad that Sally had brought her over. She smiled at him, as anyone would on being introduced and engaging in small banter. And yet to Oscar, distraught as he was, that smile conveyed more than politeness. It was an intimation.

His mind was still turned upward, conjuring up the smile with which Eros Adrestia had acknowledged Sally's introduction and guidance.

She had gone on to thank Oscar in advance for his assistance. "I'm spending some time on the coast, and I thought before returning home I'd drive down to Rhode Island and hunt up my ancestors. But the person I spoke to at Township Hall didn't seem to know her way around. Luckily I was,"—she laughed—"rescued."

"I've been here my whole life, so I knew I could help," Sally said to Oscar. Then she took Mathew's hand and led him off to the kitchen for some cookies.

Oscar was still flustered. He hadn't felt this way since he had met Danitha at The Joint, which was a college hangout for young adults who wanted to roller skate. "I'll be glad to assist you any way I can, Eros Adrestia. Do sit down."

She settled immediately into the nearest recliner, her elbows reposing on the arms, her hands in her lap. She looked at ease, happy to be relaxing.

But Oscar was shaken. He had chosen Danitha's chair. No one who came to Prudence these days ever chose it, remembering Danitha sitting there by the fire with the dogs at her feet. Not that Oscar wished it to be preserved inviolate. He abhorred sentimental rubbish like that. The only thing that irked him more was the statue in the barn. Yet as he settled himself in his own chair, he suddenly couldn't think of anything to say.

His visitor didn't seem to be expecting immediate conversation. She was looking around the room, at the shelves of books, stacked clear to the ceiling, at Danitha's portrait over the mantel and at the paintings on the walls. She faced the large fish tank in back of the room now next to a makeshift computer desk, with technology Oscar rarely found himself touching. "Cozy," she said. "That sampler!" she then exclaimed. "It must be at least a century old."

"Older. My grandmother made it at the age of eight. She was all alone, had nobody to keep her company when she came home from school. My great grandfather had gone off to do his part in World War One. So she needed a hobby. The date's in the lower right-hand corner. 1917."

Eros got up and went over to the wall where the sampler hung in a narrow gilt frame, and read aloud, "Walk cheerfully over the world, answering that of God in every one." Words so familiar to Quakers, yet they were evidently new to her, for she read the text twice.

Oscar took this opportunity to recover his composure and take in her appearance, from the blue blouse, open at the throat, to the white skirt, which fell just over her knees. Even though she'd spent the past week in town, her arms and legs were tanned. She was wearing a wedding ring. Was her husband waiting for her back home? Oscar was curious.

She, it appeared, was curious, also. "Do you own or rent?"

Oscar explained that the farmhouse in Prudence had come down to him from his grandmother, the one whose portrait hung near the fireplace. "Actually, she left Prudence to all her descendents, but I was the only one willing to beachcomb and farm. So it came to me, along with her red hair. Since the residents here are descendents of Early Quakers, dating as far back as William Penn, eight landowners across the glade share in the facilities that this region has to offer. For example, there is an estuary and a pond. The estuary is equipped with spigots, meters, and its very own filtration system. This is where we get our drinking water, and the pond is where some of us engage in light fishing and sailing. The township relies on its own water source."

"Red hair." Eros laughed, then sat down again. "For a moment I thought I was glancing at strawberry blonde."

"Small hints. That's the color my hair used to be," Oscar amended quickly, so she wouldn't think he had illusions about his appearance. "Now I'm old and crinkly with age. I admit I'm no spring chicken."

She picked up a picture frame from a nearby table. "And who is this lovely young woman? It appears she has strawberry blonde hair."

"That is my daughter."

"She lives in Prudence?" Eros asked.

"No. Connecticut."

"She's lovely."

"Yes. Beautiful, not just in appearance but in spirit. Danitha and I were so surprised when she turned out as beautiful as she did. We tried to force her into modeling, but she wasn't having it. We'd been out of touch with her—you know how these things happen in families—and she left here for her boyfriend, a city fellow, and they did not want to commit to a Quaker wedding. They wanted to go about things their own way. You know how young people are. Her boyfriend was a musician who had a fellowship for graduate study but worked days as a barista—not sure if that's what he still does—and Amy pursued a grant from the Museum of Contemporary Art to assist me with the book I was writing. That's where I get my attraction for mythology. After Danitha passed, I never had the courage to go back on that computer for more than five minutes at a time. And as Danitha is gone, it seemed natural to invite her—"

"You wrote a book?" Eros broke in.

He ignored the question. Did she think that because he was a sailor and a farmer with Quaker roots he couldn't write about Greek myth and art?

"It seemed natural," Oscar repeated, only more brusquely, "to invite her and this boyfriend of hers to make their home with me, since Amy was already in Connecticut and could commute half of the year to the university. For their part, they offered to take over the housekeeping and some of the chores. We only expected to do this till my book was finished, but then their credit card expenses sidetracked them, and they stayed. I understood completely, and said whenever you have time, email me the notes for my book. But I don't use emails, Facebook, rely on mobile phones or word processing. Half the time I disconnect my landline. It's been years now. I can't complain. I've had care and loving companionship. They've got their own life."

"Well, whatever you call this mindset of yours, do continue," Eros urged. "It's so important for a gentleman your age to get out. The writing will always be there. You will get back to it. I still remember how frustrated I was when the kids were small. I pined all day for adult conversation. My husband refused to let me work a day job. He was insistent on supporting me, so homemaker it was. My mother told me to keep my mouth shut and not complain so much, that I should be happy that I have someone to provide for me. It wasn't till my husband died and I went back to school, preparing to support my family, that I really felt fulfilled. And as somebody who had grown up around museums, a part of me had always loved classical history."

Oscar was shocked. "Fulfilled?" The word had escaped. He wanted to bite his tongue. How could a woman feel fulfilled by her husband's death?

"Yes," she said calmly, not perceiving his reaction. "I'd always wanted to curate. At the ripe age of forty I got my Ph.D. in European history and comparative mythology."

"If Amy keeps going," Oscar remarked, "she'll still be in her thirties when she gets her doctorate."

"It's harder later, I can tell you. But I worked. My husband died young, so I was left with little choice in the matter. Eventually I became dean of studies." She said it modestly, not to impress him, merely to support her contention. "I always used to tell my fellow woman students to fight for their careers. Sounds disgustingly aggressive," she acknowledged, "but in a man's world how else will they ever overcome masculine domination."

She almost made Oscar feel guilty for being a man. Hadn't Quakers always upheld the equality of the sexes?

"I do hope," she told him, "that somebody can stay with you till Amy finishes her education."

"As far as I'm concerned, it would be ideal if they stayed forever," Oscar exclaimed. "Someday I'll have to give up farming. My back and my bones aren't what they used to be.

But who'll care for this side of Prudence then? Farming's not for her."

"Naturally," Eros said, crossing her legs.

In the light they were the color of honey. Oscar thought of himself as a gentleman of the old school, though not stuffy and seldom critical of others—only demanding of himself the behavior that had been drilled into his generation. Now, thoroughly fascinated, he was unashamedly studying a strange woman's legs.

Suddenly he looked up with a start. The legs had changed position; their owner must be aware of his interest. Yes, she was watching him. He was embarrassed.

"About your Quaker ancestors," he said quickly, blushing. "What were their names?"

She gave up a few names along with a story of 19th century migration. "Mother used to tell me the frontier stories that were handed down to her, but I never paid much attention," she confessed, laughing. "It's strange, since I eventually became an historian. Now my daughter-in-law, Julia Ann, wants to know about these ancestors. She's making a family tree for my grandchildren. I can't believe my two sons will never want to look at a family tree. All they care about is sports. But I don't want to ignore my daughter-in-law's wishes." She looked at some more picture frames. "This is Danitha? She was your wife?"

"She was an artist. My grandmother did those paintings by the fireplace, but along the staircase," Oscar said, standing and waving his hand across the banister, "these oils and acrylics were done by her."

He hoped she would ask more about Danitha. But she didn't. Reluctantly he returned to the subject of Quaker heritage. "I'm sorry that Township Hall's records proved fruitless," he said. "With a little patience, you might track down your great-great-grandparents. In the early days of Prudence people didn't keep membership lists. They figured anybody could spot a Quaker by his or her speech and dress. But they kept careful records of their meetings for business, and if your forebears were active in business transactions, they might be mentioned in one of the old minute books at the community meetinghouse."

"Is the meetinghouse far from here?"

"Ten miles. I'd be glad to take you someday."

She looked at him eagerly. "Would you?"

# # #

Rowing idly, lost in recollection, Oscar was carried to the south shore of Tranquility Pond. Lottie didn't wait for him to beach the boat but jumped out and splashed up the bank. Dodo gazed apprehensively over the side. "Soon as I take my sneakers off," Oscar promised, "I'll take you ashore." These days, getting shod and unshod was proving increasingly difficult. Oscar's feet seemed to be getting farther from his arms.

At last he stood up, barefoot, and stepped into the warm water, with Dodo on his hip. The mud of the flats squished his toes until he reached dry sand. Taking care not to crush the silver clumps of dusty miller, he climbed to the top of the dune and stood still.

Before him spread an inlet to an even wider expanse of ocean. As the waves rolled in from the horizon and broke along the sunny beach, the world seemed refreshed and new, a part of it just coming into being.

The beauty of it all, of the hummingbirds from one side and the black-tailed gulls from the other, the natural expanse of the tall and thin trees, the stillness of the pond, the dunes and the ever-changing Atlantic had nourished Oscar all his life. Yet now, thinking of Eros, he found the world even more beautiful. Part of him wanted to shout her name from the top of the highest dune, another part of him refused to. She would enjoy standing here, she who had once been a homemaker and came from a landlocked town.

"I can't do it," he told himself. "I just can't."

What was it that drew him to this stranger who, unannounced, had suddenly appeared in Prudence? No one could be more unlike Danitha? His wife had never tried to manage anybody, whereas this woman, in a well-bred yet overpowering way, betrayed the norms and wielded vast knowledge in that pretty head of hers. Yet there was something in her eyes, in her manner, that seemed to contradict this, to cry out for a different fulfillment she'd missed. This hunger touched Oscar, but how was he to betray Danitha? He couldn't possibly start over, could he? Such a thought was out of the question for a man who so loved his wife that when she died he felt as if he had suffered an amputation.

Suddenly the waves in front of him settled and a small area of water started bubbling. Froth appeared at the surface of this section of sea about thirty feet away from where Oscar was standing. An ominous ringing took over his ears; at one point the ringing was so powerful that he could not hear his surroundings. Lottie and Dodo ran back toward the pond. Dogs were known to have much more sensitive ears than humans, and he had never seen the animals this spooked.

At first, Oscar thought these bubbles to be the playful work of a giant jellyfish. Jellyfish were known to gravitate near Prudence's shores, especially during morning hours. But then he saw the Barn Cupid emerge from the froth, covered in seaweed. The statue was no longer on the farm, but alive and well on this beach. He carried his signature bow, with a half full quiver of arrows on his backside. For a brief moment, at a short distance, Oscar made eye contact with the cupid. Then the statue started walking slow but mechanical like toward the shore, splashing water heavily.

"Impossible! Not real!" Oscar shouted, falling backwards in the sand. "You stay away from me! You go back to the barn! I told you, I refuse to fall in love again!"

"What are you so scared of?" the cupid asked, without even moving its mouth. It must have been communicating to Oscar telepathically.

"I'm not afraid of anything. I just don't want to betray my feelings, my Danitha."

"But Danitha knew well she was not long for this earth. That is why she hired a particular artist to sculpt me. She had me crafted for you. She had me infused with magic so you would have a guide and not be alone in this life."

Oscar lifted himself up and ran down the beach. The thought of moving on was so devastating that he failed to see an oncoming patch of barbed wire until it was almost upon him. The barbed wire separated certain sections of beach and properties that were off limits. He just missed landing in a ditch as he swerved to avoid it. Realizing how narrowly he had escaped disaster, Oscar was mortified that he should nearly have an accident because he was dreaming about a woman. And not Danitha, but another woman—one so unlike his wife that it was almost as if Oscar had become another person. But I feel just the same! I am the same! Only, he thought wryly, I'm falling in love.

He quickly made for the highest dune. Perhaps if he hid behind it, he could get away from the frightening statue that trudged slowly up the beach.

The Barn Cupid had its bow drawn and scanned the area. "Tell me, Oscar. Does not every woman bring out a different side of a man's character?" he asked, his mouth not moving. "Does your heart not ache? You are obviously a man who is somewhat at war with himself, divided in mind and heart, though you speak with such assurance that you probably aren't even aware of that part of yourself that aches."

What purpose did this talk serve? Was it to reconcile the opposing forces of nature that he longed to take Eros in his arms? But she's not my wife! How can I feel that way about someone I scarcely know? The terror of Danitha dying in front of him, that losing a loved one is so very real, the nightmares and sleepless nights that followed, the outrageous thoughts—surely these were just caused by some momentary aberration that would never come again.

Sensing Oscar's anxiety, the Barn Cupid took to reassuring him. "Your readiness to respond to a cry for recognition is both touching and grand," it said. "It has the authentic ring of what you Quakers call a leading. But it is also troubling, confusing." A part of Oscar hoped the cupid would continue this narrative. But the statue showed no inclination to go on.

Instead, he said, "You humans. It's charming, your plain body language. It's the same language in which my race made their marriage promises. So I am quite familiar with it. When mortals come seeking my help, I slip naturally into responding. It's especially gratifying to me because my race revolted against the body language. The gods laughed when they heard me speaking of love, and they have never overcome their aversion for it."

"This isn't some myth! Danitha's death changed my whole life!" Oscar yelled out, ducking. "It changed my entire perspective! All the plans I had for our retirement, all the places in the world we wanted to visit, all the things we'd been looking forward to doing—death crowded out everything." Oscar stopped briefly. "How contrary life is," he muttered on. "Your race have the right to say this and that, but doesn't necessarily have to act, while I—it makes me wish I hadn't fallen in love in the first place."

"Then let me fix that," offered the cupid.

"No. Don't you dare! You stay away from me." Oscar ran out from his hiding place and tried to escape the nearing statue. As soon as he reached the opposite end of the beach, near the docks, the cupid removed its laurel and it became a small bolo whip made of blinding light. He swung the bolo whip around his stone head and launched it. It wrapped itself around Oscar's legs, causing the old widower to immediately drop face first to the sand.

A moment later the Barn Cupid stood over him.

"Be still and cool," Oscar said, looking up at his stony glare. "Be still and cool in thy own mind and spirit from thy own thoughts."

"This will only hurt for a moment," the cupid said, pulling back on the bow and aiming just below Oscar's ribcage.

"Here it comes," Oscar went on nervously. "Be still and cool in thy own mind and spirit from thy own thoughts. Then thou wilt feel the principle of God to turn thy mind to, whereby thou wilt receive his strength and power from whence life comes, to allay all tempests—"

The arrow punctured skin. Oscar screamed in hot pain.

Looking down at his abdomen he saw a pool of dark blood form. The experience had shaken him. So much so that he felt woozy. But by the time the statue had returned to the watery depths from whence it came, the blood that had leaked out had done a quick reverse back, and the wound had become nothing more than an artificial scrape. It was almost as if he had never been injured.

"When the time is right," the statue telepathically echoed out, words reverberating in Oscar's hazy mind, "bring the woman to me. Then, and only then, shall the union be complete."

Now standing up in the sand, hand clutched to his side and facing the ocean, Oscar recollected Eros's mannerisms. There had been a hint of playfulness in her walk and a hint of wistfulness in her voice that had gone straight to his heart. And this feeling! What was this feeling that was beginning to overwhelm him? Almost instantly a strange emotion gripped his body and held it fast.

Oscar felt blessedly calm now. He hadn't, after all, lost control of his mind. He was all right, and his heart wasn't damaged. He looked at his wrinkly hands. He thought with amusement that life would have been simpler if, as his joints aged, his feelings had also. But he still craved the companionship of a charming woman.

He whistled. "Lottie! Dodo! Where are you?" He hurried back to the boat. "Now where did those dogs get to? I have a phone call to make."

Until Eros appeared, his future had seemed predictable— your typical widower's tale, a continuation, at best, of the present, with his powers slowly diminishing. Now, anything might happen. The possibility filled him with alarm. And yet it was invigorating, too. Disparate though they were, he and Eros shared an essential quality. They were both what members of the Quaker community called seekers, open to leadings of the spirit.

# # #

Eros Adrestia remembered that about twenty miles east of Prudence, between Bristol and Kensington, a double row of maples lined the main road for six tenths of a mile. Just beyond the maples a road had branched off on the left, zigzagging toward the upper end of Tranquility Pond. Little more than a sandy trail covered with broken scallop shells, it petered out in front of a rural mailbox marked by eight properties and the words PRUDENCE FARM.

When the line of maples finally disappeared and Eros started to drive under the last of the leafy arches, she caught her breath. She was proceeding under a shimmering canopy of new nature, the likes she'd never seen, with sunlight filtering through leaves of scarlet and gold. The road was a portal through which she had passed into a world of unsuspected enchantment.

Jewels of leaves fell carelessly onto the hood of the Volkswagen, a sign that autumn wasn't too far off. Leaning out of the window, Eros laughed as whirls of color, blowing past, almost touched her cheek. Then she reproached herself for letting her tires mash the red and brown carpet, flecked with gold, that seemed to have been rolled out in welcome. The world she was entering, she thought happily, was unlike any she'd ever known, a world in which goodness took precedence over success, and gentleness prevailed.

At Prudence there was an almost palpable beauty. There was calm, not inactivity, and an awareness of unfailing security; the doors were never locked. Yet the man who communicated all this was completely human, chock full of idiosyncrasies, brimming over with humor and, at the same time, possessed of a self-knowledge that awed Eros. Prudence was a revelation, the antithesis of the world she'd frantically pushed through during all her working life.

When Oscar finally did call on the pretext of sharing his news, things had turned out far better than she'd expected. Oscar expressing his feelings to her had provided a great opening, and she had grabbed it. She searched inside herself. She knew she harbored the same feelings Oscar did, for weeks now. She just didn't want to admit it.

But now that she was nearly there, Eros wondered whether she would be up to taking care of a man again. She was unusually well and energetic. Still, there were days when aches and pains gripped her—nothing major, just enough to make her aware of her age. Furthermore, on her last visit Oscar had feared her. There was a difference between something expressed over the phone and something said face to face. Would he finally be transparent with her?

One thing about Oscar, he was very gracious, listening to her with extraordinary interest, as if what she was saying mattered wholly to him. Although he communicated to her with a certain warmth that in another man might have signified special affection, Eros Adrestia knew that she meant no more to Oscar Heartdale than anyone else. Besides, it wasn't Oscar, she assured herself, but the whole ambience of the glade that attracted her—the red barn, the silo in back, the estuary and fishing pond, the old white farmhouse.

Now, as she drew up beside the horse block and stopped the motor, she saw him standing in the doorway, tall and erect. All at once it dawned on her that with all its beauty, it wasn't Prudence that drew her back so forcefully. It was Oscar. It was love.

The realization proved so upsetting to her that she lost her poise, and instead of returning to Oscar's greeting as he hurried toward her, she blurted out, "What's for lunch?" What a betrayal of anxiety.

Opening the car door and smiling down on her, Oscar answered, "It's in the oven." Then, as he always did when there was a guest, Oscar said cordially, "Welcome to Prudence Farm." He lifted her bag out of the car.

She found herself standing in the driveway, taking his outstretched hand and meeting his blue eyes, which were unmistakably joyful. She wanted to tell him about the splendor of the maples along the road. Yet no words came. As he stood aside to let her enter the house, she wondered, What's the matter with me? I've always been self-possessed. Suddenly I'm acting like a giddy teenager. Then the gracious entrance hall enfolded her, and she felt better.

"If you're thirsty I have a pitcher of lemonade," Oscar said, leading her into the living room. He put the bag down. "By the way, maybe when we're done eating, I can show you something in the barn."

This stopped Eros. "Oh? What?"

"Something a historian like yourself would greatly appreciate. It's special to me, and I think you'll find it special too."

"Why not?" Eros looked touched. "I've been thinking about you."

Oscar went to turn off the stove. "And I've been thinking about you," he said.

When he came back, he picked Eros's bag back up, led the way upstairs and across the landing to the ell, explaining a bit breathlessly about his situation. "This feeling I have inside me surprises me too much," he admitted. "That is why I couldn't hold it in. I had to call you up. I needed to hear your voice. Just before Danitha died, I felt a similar emotion. On her deathbed, she would tell me how I lovingly took care of her, and how I should have been a nurse. Imagine that, a crotchety old fool like me a nurse. Danitha always said my nursing gave her a feeling of doing something special for someone in need. While much of what she did on the farm could just as well be done by a machine, she knew how much I despised electronics. So she hired outside help. One of the people she hired was a mysterious sculptor. He flew here all the way from Greece."

"Did he paint portraits when your wife was ill?" Eros asked.

"No, no. Weak as she was, Danitha still managed her painting from bed."

"What do you think these feelings really mean to you?"

Oscar seemed baffled. "As a woman, I thought you might know better." He dare not mention the encounter with the cupid on the beach. "I confess that an undying love, a flame which cannot be put out, would have seemed more important than anything."

Eros laughed. "If you men only understood how most women feel."

Then she gave him a small peck on the lips.

The room he ushered her into was extravagant, bedspreads and furniture in the finest mahogany and royal silks. The brass bedstead, the diminutive heater, the antique clock, the makeup vanity with its dresser drawers and oval mirror, adorned with faux gemstones around the sides, the sketches covering the walls—of a little girl at six months, a year, and three or four. Oscar put her bag on the luggage rack. "The spare bathroom is down the hall. You can freshen up at that mirror," he said, finger outstretched and pointing. He started to leave.

"Are these sketches of your daughter?" Eros inquired.

"Yes. Unfinished. Danitha did them long ago." Backing into the hall, Oscar added, "Amy paid me a lovely visit last week. I have you to thank for that. I must be patient now till her next visit."

"Did Amy say anything about the book?"

"I turned the computer back on as soon as she left. I managed five pages. Not much, but something is better than nothing."

He paused.

He came in once more, and Eros watched him struggle with his words. From the back, she thought, one would never guess his age. But it was more than his beautiful façade that distinguished him. It was his bearing, the combination of dignity and humility. To Eros, these had seemed mutually exclusive. In Oscar they were clearly intertwined.

Turning from the door, he suddenly looked at Eros with a light in his eyes that she'd never seen before, as if he were about to come toward her and take her into his arms. Her heart lurched. But, of course, he did no such thing. It was just Eros's crazy imagination. Instead, he walked right past her to the windowsill, where he picked up a stone arrow. Then, as he was about to take it with him, he said apologetically, "In the excitement of your arrival, I forgot to get the table set." He finally exited.

"I'll be right down to help," she called out.

Eros turned around and noticed a yellow rose standing in a slender red vase on the bedside table. She knew Oscar had put it there. He was such a gentleman. Sniffing the delicate scent, she thought, How could I possibly feel rejected?

# # #

When Oscar spoke about his wife at the dining room table, Eros felt uncomfortable. It made her a little jealous. Her own husband slaved for her as much as anybody. She knew that. But he hadn't been capable of caring about her the way Oscar did about his wife. Danitha's charm and professional success also roused some envy in her. To be both cherished and famous—that was too much.

Eros had so wanted to be cherished. When she was young, affection and passion bubbled over in her. She had put everything into the marriage, trying to make something of her home so her husband would be proud of her. He didn't even notice. When he knew he was dying, he showed less sorrow over being separated from her than from his two cats.

She had resolved then never to risk surrendering her life again. It's not really that I'm jealous of Danitha, Eros thought. I'm glad she had Oscar's love. What hurts is that her own husband couldn't give her something like that. If he had, she would have been more content.

"Sometimes we have to give in to surrender," Oscar said over small bites of his food.

The man must be terribly lonely to say such a thing. Had he really been reading her mind?

"These petit fours are splendid," she said, looking down at her plate.

"Prudence has some of the finest confectionaries. You'll find our pastries exquisitely sweet in taste, and our bakers like none other along the coast."

"This meal was delicious," she said, putting her napkin down. "I'm busting at the seams. I should change into something a little more comfortable. You wanted to show me something in the barn?"

"Yes. I own a work of art. You must see it."

"Oh? What kind of art?" she asked.

"A statue," Oscar answered. "A teenage cherubim depicting a winged messenger of love. A lot of hours went into the making of it. It's very special."

"You know, they say cupid was seen as a good spirit who could take many forms, some subconsciously transformative. They also say he brought happiness to all, but such matchmaking in ancient times did not come without some deceptive plotting or mischief."

"They also say Venus used her son's power to get revenge on her rivals. Love is a funny thing, especially when it comes to myth. The trials and tribulations of the heart. Be careful what you wish for. You never quite know what you're going to end up with."

"True." Eros pushed her chair back. "I shall return."

After unpacking the rest of her clothes, Eros ran a comb through her hair and started to leave the room. On second thought, she decided to change from her skirt and knit top to the dress she'd brought, a soft blue-and-rose paisley print. This was her first time wearing it. It was a special occasion.

Oscar must have been listening to her footsteps, because as she crossed the landing and came down the staircase, he was waiting for her below, his shining face uplifted. There was no mistaking his impulse. His left arm was stretched out to receive her. His right arm was held behind his back, gripping the stone arrow. It was the same arrow the cupid had pierced him with on the beach.

All the way to the barn, Eros was beside herself. Oscar was awfully quiet. He didn't even want to hold her hand. The mood was peculiar until they reached the giant wood doors.

In sunshine, the barn looked even more unattractive than the last time Oscar visited it. In the bright September morning, the clear antiques and historical baubles lining the back section glinted all sorts of brown and gold. The haystacks had been removed now, and the sky above the square archway was a cloudless blue. Outside, the leaves of the trees that shaded the termite-ridden walls of the old structure were crimson, saffron, and brittle russet.

Oscar watched Eros trace the dates of each item she touched with her finger. "What do you think?" he asked.

"Disorderly." Eros was shocked, but amused. "Why?"

"As an artist, Danitha casually thought to distract guests from the main business of life, which was the cultivation of the spirit." Oscar pulled the drop cloth away from the statue. The Barn Cupid shone in the morning light. "The old Quakers were ahead of their time in many respects," he went on. "But in mythology, no. Mythology was excluded from their lives, even from their belief system. A member who happened to be present at a gathering of Greek art was termed guilty of disorderly viewing."

Eros examined the statue with excitement, as Oscar read some slanting script etched into the marble base: "That such laws of the heart be made, may true love be forever."

The scene that greeted Eros in the back of the barn was so mesmerizing as to be almost welcoming. As she touched the statue's face, Oscar just a few feet behind her, she was struck again by its austerity. No altar, no pulpit, just sunshine glowing in on this amazing sculpture. There was a reverent aura about the simple features, as if the inspirations experienced there still permeated it. But it was missing one thing. She was not sure if this was intentional on behalf of the artist, or if this feature had been removed.

"This cupid has no bow," Eros noticed. "It's holding a dagger."

"A keen observation," Oscar whispered.

Eros turned and faced him. She wanted to hug him, but he pushed her away.

"Don't you love me?" she asked with mock chagrin.

His eyes level with hers, Oscar answered unequivocally, "No." Then he stepped forward and thrust the stone arrow in her gut.

Eros's eyes opened in surprise, and she looked down at the tear in her dress and the gaping wound in her abdomen. Bleeding profusely, she fell backwards against the base of the statue.

"I could never love anybody but Danitha," Oscar said truthfully. "I know this. Prudence knows this. Danitha was aware of this." He looked up at the Barn Cupid, who was starting to come to life. "I told you back at the house. Sometimes you have to give in to surrender." He took a step back. "The crucial test of love is whether certain feelings can regenerate old life into others."

The Barn Cupid put its thick stony arm around Eros's neck, picking her up halfway off the floor. Then he took the dagger and stabbed her in the chest with it. Eros gasped for air and let out a barely audible scream. A moment later the cupid dropped her lifeless body to the ground where light flooded out of her wounds. Soon new light flooded into every crevice of her body, and her form changed instantly. Where Eros's body had once been was now Danitha Heartdale's body.

After that, the whole scene became blurred. Danitha's face, having replaced Eros's face, lit up. "She was a good soul. She put up cheerfully with the transition. Then the old soul left." In spite of her gloom, and needing a corporeal form, Danitha enjoyed her resurrection, and treasured being reunited with Oscar.

"I'm here to stay," she said.

"I know," Oscar said, smiling.

"I'm not going anywhere ever again. I promise you."

"We'll be together forever and ever."

"Till death do us part again."

Oscar put his hand on her cheek. "Till death do us part again." He felt her affection reaching out. A wave of sympathetic amusement rippled over the barn.

"I knew we couldn't do it without divine assistance," she said. "Because doing what you feel is right sometimes means taking risks."

Barely able to contain his joy, Oscar said, "My whole life has been a continuum of love. You have been a part of that continuum."

Looking as if she might break down any minute in this new body, Danitha said, "I think it's even more wonderful for old people—who know how rough death can be—to make this commitment." She turned to him with a radiant smile.

We may not have many years, Oscar conceded to himself, as he and Danitha walked jubilantly out of the barn together, while the statue lingered in the silence. But love isn't measured by time. It is measured by legacy, and it may be the only thing in the universe that lives forever.

"So, wait, you're saying one of these… these 'Cupids' can resurrect the dead?" It was only a story, he knew, but not one he'd heard ever associated with this particular myth. The association of the two disparate ideas was off-putting somehow, mentally discomfiting.

Hiram smiled a thin smile as he put a heavy utility blanket over the statue. "All gods have some level of dominion over life and death. More if that control happens to overlap with their ordained purview." The statue safely draped, the old proprietor began ambling down one of the aisle of overcrowded shelves. "And who wouldn't do just about anything to return a loved one to this mortal plane? Orpheus and Eurydice, remember? Tale as old as time itself."

Thunder shook the room, reminding Kevin of the torrential downpour that kept him an unwitting captive in the curious shop. "I guess," he replied, trying his best to sound as though he understood. "I mean, death, and whatever happens after that, it's been the eternal mystery, right?"

The older man turned abruptly, a gleam in his eye. In his hands he held a blown-glass object, shaped like a valentine. "A mystery?" he said cheerfully. "Yes, I suppose it is, for many. A mystery to be solved." He brought the glass valentine to his eye like a magnifying glass. "Sounds like something for a good detective to get involved with."

The Nick Victory Chronicles
Part Five: Heart of Glass

By Paul Barile

The joint was filled with every knick-knack and doo-dad and goo-gaw you could imagine. I never seen nothing like it in my life. Sabre heard about it on the radio and decided it would be a good place to unwind after all we been though.

I was never much for goo-gaws or doo-dads, but Sabre can't resist 'em. Sabre gives it his all - all the time - so if he wants to see something – who am I to knock it. I can't deny the guy.

So, there we were in aisle after aisle of switchblade combs and X-ray specs. That's when Sabre saw the sign directing saps to the Carnival Glass. He looked at the sign – then he looked at me.

"Nicky," he said.

"Go ahead," I said.

He smiled.

I smiled.

He disappeared into the maze of wood shelves holding vases and platters and all the stuff you can win at the midway if you can throw a dart or a baseball. That wasn't my scene – but if Sabre liked it – I figured it had to be jake.

I didn't really need nothing except a breath of fresh air so I headed back to the front door.

"Nothing catch your eye, Boyo?" the guy behind the counter asked.

"I have everything I want and I want everything I have," I answered. I can get deep.

I looked the guy over. He was kinda familiar, but I never been in this joint before. I seen a big fat housefly just above the guy's eyebrow. The guy seemed oblivious to it and the fly never moved. He clung to that guy's forehead like a fat guy with a pork chop.

I couldn't believe it. The guy went back to his newspaper –
flipping the pages – not reading so much as fanning himself.
The fly never moved. I walked out after wishing both of
them a good day.

When Sabre found me outside, he had a brown paper bag
in his hand and a smile on his face.

"Did you see that fly?" he asked.

"I did."

We laughed.

We headed back towards the flat. Sabre didn't show me
what was in the bag and I didn't ask. I got a gold medal
in minding my own business – and that bag was none of
my business.

We walked into the flat and he walked right into the kitchen
as he does. The great chefs of the world could take tips from
Sabre Bratcher. I grabbed the newspaper and was about to sit
down when the headline jumped right off the page.

HEARTBREAK KILLER STRIKES AGAIN

I didn't need to read the words to know what was up. The
Heartbreak Killer was my nemesis. He'd been quiet for almost
a year and now he was back.

The Heartbreak Killer was known for killing grooms on
their wedding day. The coppers typically found them
somewhere between their house and the church and when
they did find 'em, they had a red carnation in his mouth.

The smell coming out of the kitchen drew me in like a
cartoon wolf catching a pie off a window sill. What I saw
there was artful – even for Sabre.

"What gives?" I asked.

"It's your surprise birthday dinner," he laughed.

"My birthday is next week."

"That's why it's a surprise."

Who was I to argue? I grabbed a seat and Sabre piled
my plate high with calamari marinara and linguine. It
really is my favorite birthday dinner. I dug in like a sailor
on leave. I forgot to put the napkin in my shirt collar like
a proper gentleman.

"Nick, please don't let the newspaper spoil your surprise birthday dinner." Sabre said.

"Fair enough," I said.

I didn't even slow down. Each slurp of pasta slapped my chin – warm and satisfying.

"After we eat, I have a present for you."

I kept shoveling the calamari in like it was my job. Between the slurping and the crunching, I cursed only one birthday dinner a year. No one I know – not even my old Nana could make garlic bread the way old Sabre did. It was crispy and crunchy on the outside and soft as a warm marshmallow on the inside. It just melted in my gullet.

"We gotta get this guy." I said while I was sopping the last of the marinara with the last of the garlic bread.

"We will, Nicky."

"We will," I said. "Now where's my gift."

Sabre left the kitchen for a second. He's going to make someone a good mate someday. He really is a good egg.

He came back in and handed me the bag from the goo-gaw store. I took it and tested the heft in my hand. It wasn't a muffin and it wasn't a brick. I opened the bag like little Jack Horner only I pulled out a smooth glass heart.

"Thanks, old chum," I said. "It's beautiful."

Just as I was about to close the bag, a fly buzzed out of it and did a lap around the room before settling on my good fedora that was hanging on a hook by the door.

"This heart will make your dreams come true. All of them." Sabre said.

He was really into it and I didn't feel the need to rain on his parade so I just went with it. I ain't much of a dreamer – and I never expect anything from anyone any time. He just looked so happy about it. I set the glass heart on the table and took a long look at it.

"Tomorrow, we start looking for the Heartbreak Killer," I said. "Tonight, we sleep the good sleep."

And we did.

Come morning Sabre was already making coffee and eggs. I went down to get my paper from the old doorman who had jokes so bad they pealed the paint.

"Hey Nicky," Chet crowed. "What do you put in a bucket to make it lighter?"

"A hole," a voice behind me answered.

I turned around to see a dame guys like me only dream about. Deep red hair rolled up in a perfect coif like a space helmet in an old sci-fi film — but somehow it worked. Her eyes were slate blue like the sky before a storm. Her skin was her sin — it was porcelain — I was in. Don't even get me started on the gams.

My jaw dropped. She musta caught that because she took her two perfect fingers under my chin and pushed my yap shut.

"You must be Nick Victory," she said.

"I must be," I responded the words thick in my throat.

"I'm Adelaide — Adelaide Sinclair. I was hoping to find you here."

"Me, too."

"Is there somewhere we can talk?"

Chet just stared at us. He was frozen like a snowman in an old tuxedo.

"Let's go upstairs," I finally said.

"I'm right behind you."

We took the elevator. There was no talking on the ride, but there was a lot of smelling. I never got myself trapped in an elevator with a dame who smelled like a fresh lilac. There was no way I was going to talk and distract myself from embedding this ride in my memory.

Sabre was still cooking when we walked back into the apartment. He just pulled out another plate and another cup for coffee.

"Oh, I can't stay long," she said. "I just — well — I've heard so much about you and I really wanted to meet you.

While she was talking — she was looking around the room like she lost something and she was anxious to find it. When she spotted the glass heart, she reached for it. She was just about to lay her perfect mitt on it when that fly swooped down and kamikazed her. She jumped back a moment, but he took another dive straight at her.

For a brief moment – Adelaide Sinclair looked like a regular human being. She looked normal – not like a goddess. I felt sorry for her, but the fly didn't. He swooped one more time and Adelaide Sinclair scurried out the door faster than you can say Sweet Mama's Pajamas taking her perfect lilac perfume with her.

After breakfast, Sabre and I hit the streets. The Heartbreak Killer was a serious piece of work, but so was I. We started our careers at around the same time, only I was a good guy and he was the devil.

Sabre and I decided to start at the parking garage by the opera house. That was where the final victim was found. We thought we'd canvas the area and see if we had any better luck than the last time – or the time before.

We hopped off the bus at Monroe and hoofed it down to Wabash and into the driveway that led to the garage. We got to the lobby to chat with the attendant when I bumped into a cute doll waiting for her car. She was no Adelaide Sinclair – but she was cute. I like cute.

"Do I know you?" she asked.

"I don't think so," I said.

"Are you sure?"

"I'm pretty sure, Miss."

"Why don't you take my number and call me when you figure it out?" she asked with a smile.

This had to be a grift. I normally couldn't meet a girl with a double-sawbuck stapled to my fedora

"Call any time. Any time at all. I'll be there."

Her car pulled up the curb. The jockey got out and she slid in to the driver's seat. She winked at me before pulling out of the driveway and going south on Wabash. I looked at Sabre.

"Was that-"

"Yeah, that was weird," Sabre said.

I didn't notice the fly buzzing around my head.

The car jockey startled me when he came around the

corner. He was looking down and I was looking out when we bumped into each other.

"What can I do ya' for? Art museum? Tea Room?"

"Just a few questions," I said.

"Shoot. I only got a minute – but maybe I can help."

"This is the last place the Heartbreak Killer struck. Were you working that day?"

"Of course. I work every day."

"Did you see anything?"

"Nah. Like I told the police – when I came down from parkin' some stiff's Buick, the guy was sitting in that chair – right by the head. He was wearing a tux. I thought he passed out from too much ocky-docky."

I looked at Sabre.

"Drinking," the guy said, "Ain't you got no culture?"

"Do you remember anything else? Is there anything you can think of that you – maybe - forgot to tell the police?"

"Now that you mention it," he started. He rubbed his chin like it might provoke a thought. "The smell."

"Because he was by the bathroom?"

"No, Sport. Just a smell. The place smelled like an orchid or maybe a daisy. You know - like women's bathwater."

I looked at Sabre. He looked at me. We both looked back at the car jockey.

"One more thing," he said. "He didn't even have a car so why was he in here in the first place?"

I looked at Sabre. He looked at me. We both looked back at the car jockey.

"If I figure that out – I'll let you know."

And just that quick we were back on the street.

"How about the bowling alley?" Sabre asked.

We walked out to State Street and down the stairs.

The red line gets packed in the middle of the day with the kids going to class or to work. It's clean but a little tight. I was surprised to find a seat. There was a woman sitting by the window so I sat down next to her.

Sabre sat up front by the engineer door. He likes the view – he said he feels like he's the driver looking down the tunnel like that.

The woman turned to me and smiled. I smiled back. Her hair was so black it was blue like in the funnies. Her eyes were green fire – lighting up her flawless skin. I swallowed hard and she must have noticed it because she smiled.

"I'm Agnessa," she said.

"Uh… Nick. Nick Victory."

"I've never seen you on this train. Are you heading to work?"

"No, ma'am. I'm already kinda working."

"You have a handsome smile, Nick Victory. Your jaw is strong."

I was sweating in places I didn't even know I had glands. It was all I could do to not slide out of that seat. I was slicker than a spitball in July.

"Thank you."

"I don't want to be too forward, but I get off at the next stop. I would never forgive myself if I didn't give you my number. We really should spend some time getting to know each other."

She made me dizzy. My gut was flipping like a fat kid on a trampoline. Since when am I the hottest ticket in town?

She slipped me her number as she slowly stepped over me – letting me know she was stepping over me slowly. She arched her back as she made out of the seat and into the aisle in time for the screeching brakes and the sliding doors.

I looked at that slip of paper so intently I didn't even notice the fly sitting on my finger.

The bowling alley was full of greasers and geezers and the smoke was stale. We knew the second victim was found here. It had been a while – but I know how to shake people until the truth falls out. We had to find the shoe guy. He'd know the score.

"I'm Miller," he said. He had a pair of sweaty shoes in one hand and a can of spray in the other. "I'm the one who found him."

"What do you remember about that night? Take it easy. I know it's been a while — but it looks like the killer is back and we need to catch him."

"Like I told the cops, I was in the back resetting the pin setter and when I came out — he was leaning against the popcorn machine. His head was down. I thought he was zozzled so I let him sleep it off."

"What else do you remember?"

"The smell. I won't forget the smell?"

"Flowers? Orchids?"

"Popcorn. He was leaning against the machine and that smell is everywhere. DO I need sto slow down for you?"

I handed Miller my card. Told him to not be a stranger.

Out on the street, we were busted, but it wasn't the end of the world. I had two phone numbers. That's two more numbers than I have ever gotten in my life. Things weren't jake for the investigation, but they were copasetic in other areas. I decided we need to go home and get some lunch. We had to regroup.

"Let's splurge on a cab," I said.

Sabre and I hopped into a cab and headed back to the neighborhood. We didn't talk much. I mostly stared at those beautiful digits. It was like calligraphy or something. I couldn't figure how two seven-digit numbers looked like a million bucks. The fly sat on the headrest behind the driver's head. He was rubbing his tiny mitts together. I'm pretty sure he winked at me.

The cab pulled up and we hopped out and Sabre gave the guy a nice tip. While he was paying, this pretty young co-ed strolled past us. She was one of those good things that come in small packages. Watching her walk away was like watching two puppies wrestling under a blanket.

"Like what you see?" she said barely turning her melon.

"I do," I said. Suddenly, I'm the goods. I'm chattin' this doll up and she's got no idea who I am — who I really am — so I resist the urge to be myself.

"Do something about it," she said.

That flummoxed me. Gentlemen code insists on conversation and nicey-nice. Gumshoe code says take her in my arms and kiss her hard until she stops squirming. As good as a private eye as I am – it just ain't in me to be a dick.

"Coffee?" I finally said.

When she turned around, I thought I was looking at Bettie Page's younger sister. This little lady redefined robust in all the right ways. Her hair shimmered in the sun like Lake Placid. He eyes sparkled like ice cubes. I was gobsmacked.

"Tea?" she asked, making her way back toward me.

"Anything you like," I said. "Let's go upstairs."

Sabre went in first – then the dame – then the fly – then me.

As soon as I opened the door, I knew there was going to be trouble. The room reeked of lilacs – it took me a minute to realize that Adelaide Sinclair was there – or had been there recently.

"Take my wrap?" the young dame said pulling her angora sweater off her soft shoulder.

I grabbed it hung it on the coat rack – next to my fedora. The fly took a seat on the sweater and watched as the fireworks began.

Suddenly and without warning - Adelaide Sinclair ran out of the bedroom gunning for Sabre like she's Dick Butkus. She was screaming and the young dame was screaming and Sabre was trying to scream, but it's caught in his throat.

"WHERE IS IT?" Adelaide Sinclair screamed.

"What? What?" Sabre couldn't yell – but she heard him.

"Where's the heart?"

"What heart?"

"The heart you bought from the old Greek, Hiram. Where is it?"

"It's just a piece of carnival glass."

"It's my piece pf carnival glass you son of a-"

"Watch it sister," I said reaching for my gat.

The young dame hid behind the couch and watched as Adelaide Sinclair lunged at Sabre again. He looked toward kitchen. She caught him looking toward the kitchen and jumped like her ass was on fire.

Sabre made the first move – but she was quicker. She grabbed the heart and held it over her head like Lady Liberty. The young dame looked at her. I looked at her. Sabre looked at her. I looked at Sabre. Then we all looked at Adelaide Sinclair and that carnival glass heart she was brandishing.

She stalked back into the front room holding the glass heart high over her head. Her eyes were wild and her mouth was a disfigured gash.

"Drop it," I said.

"All I wanted was my own happily ever after. I wanted my white picket fence. I just wanted one true love. What did I get? I got bupkis. Someone has to pay. They all have to pay," Adelaid said.

That's when I realized who she was. The Heartbreak Killer wasn't a cat – it was a chick. She was a chick. The Heartbreak Killer was of the female persuasion. There she was in my flat.

Suddenly she slammed that hunk of glass down like a sudden death touchdown in Soldier Field.

The sound was deafening and the lights were piercing. Beams of light shot in every direction – then there wasn't a sound. It was so quiet – I thought for a minute my ears were broke. The young dame came to me like I was going to save her. I wrapped my arm around her while I kept the gat trained on Adelaide Sinclair.

Then we heard it. It was the softest pop you ever heard. The pop was followed by a small breathless moan. The fly fell to the ground. His days of buzzing around us were over. I had no idea how sad a moment could be.

In all of the commotion, Adelaide Sinclair hit the bricks. I looked down at my little friend. When I looked back at the young dame, she started coughing.

"I need to go do some laundry," she said. She grabbed her sweater she bolted out the door and down the stairs.

"I'll get a broom." Sabre said.

He left me alone with a pile of broken carnival glass, a dead fly, and two phone numbers. I unfolded paper that held the first number only to see it was a shopping list from Bari's on Grand. I looked at the second piece of paper and was not surprised to see it was a receipt from the Biograph Theater.

I took the broom from Sabre and began sweeping.

"My gift. My mess."

"I don't mind, Nick."

"I got it."

Sabre disappeared into his room.

I set the broom against the back of the couch and walked over to check out the fly. I felt bad I never gave him a name, but he was good to me – until he wasn't anymore. Sometimes that's just how things go. One minute you're surrounded by goo-gaws – then you're surrounded by righteous skirts – then you're sweeping up your broken heart.

"You don't sound Greek," Kevin.

Hiram arched an eyebrow. "That's what you came away with?" He shook his head ruefully and muttered. "Prepei na leo kaliteres istories."

Kevin's mouth opened but nothing came out. The flip phone began skittering over the counter again with an insistent bzzt-bzzt. "Do you, ah, do you need to get that?"

"Hmm? Oh, that? No, that's not for me," the older man said with a dismissive wave. He produced a feather duster from nowhere, like a stage magician but without any flourish of showmanship — a prosaic trick — and began dusting his way down a shelf of books, moving the accumulations of dust from one spine to the other.

Kevin shrugged. The phone stopped buzzing. He was half-hoping the old man would have picked up the phone, had someone else to yammer at until the storm passed.

As the proprietor disappeared down the aisle, Kevin turned toward the door, and the torrents beyond it. As he turned, his elbow brushed a red glass vase that had been perched just at the lip of the shelf beside him.

"Oh cr—"

Before he could complete his exclamation, Hiram's broad hand, long fingers splayed, caught the fragile object just before it hit the bare concrete floor.

Kevin blinked twice. "How? How did you—?"

"Used to play a lot of basketball back in the day," Hiram said. "Mayan Leagues." He held the vase up to the light and peered through the glass surface, turning it about, clucking. "Good. Good. Not a scratch." He placed it back on the shelf — just as precariously close to the edge as it had been before. "Wouldn't do to go breaking this one, let me tell you."

A VASE THE COLOUR OF MISCHIEF
Tanya Delanor

It started well enough.

Raspberry-painted lips and a Chilean red. Sounds like a date. But it wasn't. Time to catch up with extended family. Mother was delighted to see her sister and co. They had moved since we last saw them, which was at Dad's funeral.

They were always moving. My Uncle Kai secured a banking position in India for a year. We could have gone for a visit, but Mother worried about the jabs we would need. Next there was Kenya, but we are not allowed to talk about that, as Uncle Kai had to leave quickly. Rumour has it that he was sacked, but each time I dare to bring it up with Mother, she gives me that look she used to give me when I was offered something to eat that she didn't think was hygienic enough. We also missed out on Uncle Kai's post a year or two later in Australia. One of my other cousins visited, and told of a scary story involving an Airbnb our Uncle Kai had booked him into. I didn't even know they did Airbnb in Australia, but it seemed I was mistaken. It's the spiders Mother couldn't abide, although she made out I was the one who was the true arachnophobe. Truth was that she was scared to death of snakes. She even had nightmares about that one. Anyway, my cousin said that when Uncle Kai showed him round the Airbnb, it looked like somebody was already staying there, and had just gone out for a few minutes.

"Don't worry 'bout it," said Uncle Kai, his pronounced philtrum now partly obscured by a wispy grey and blond moustache. "Oh, and before you mention spiders, he's got some pet ones. They won't bother you." My cousin looked up at a tall filing cabinet, which amongst other clutter had a dry aquarium pitched on its top. It looked dusty and cobwebby and the spiders clearly had the run of the room, should they so choose.

Did he go, or did he stay? I think he wimped out and booked into a hotel instead. I doubt Uncle Kai was impressed.

Because many of us didn't have cars, and the location was miles from bus and railway stations, the "Australia" cousin offered to hire an old coach to drive us all there. He insisted, saying, "The only other times we all seem to get together is because of one of the big three events, so let's do this." Mother was emphatic that she didn't want to risk her life or anybody else's by driving along "one of those STUPID motorways that they lie about being SMART," as Dad had told her it was just a cynical ruse to save money and fool drivers at the same time. He said the government were trying to deal with the increase in road traffic without being mindful of safety. He heard somewhere that the powers-that-be didn't reckon ordinary folk would have the nerve to sue over accidents due to these STUPID motorways. In Dad's memory, we all voted to play SAFE not STUPID and chose the scenic route instead.

The journey was hot, bumpy, and nausea-inducing for one of the kids. Toilet stops were infrequent and usually meant the desperate had to sneak in the undergrowth to relieve themselves. I felt sorry for Mother, as she had roughed it most of her life, had rheumatoid arthritis, and was only just getting used to her own indoor toilet and central heating.

We arrived to find a big old house in the country surrounded by fields and huge skies. Uncle Kai's 4x4 was parked in front. He was leaning over it, polishing the metal bits. When he saw us appearing, he half-waved by flicking the duster at us, and then stood hands on hips while my cousin rattled and gear-scraped the aged coach into a parking position.

"Ooh," we sang in unison as we dismounted.

The children ran round and round outside, while the adults entered the dining room and fussed over food. Mother began a discussion which bored me, so I retreated to the kitchen. It was smaller than I expected. No free working surface. Somebody had emptied the dishwasher but left all the clean crockery out. I reached towards a green-stemmed wine glass, and that's when the dish tumbled. I made a half-hearted attempt to break its fall. It was blue and gold and looked vintage. When it fell, it made no sound at all, and I thought all was well. But when I picked it up, it was broken in half, and the handle had snapped off. It must have been a wide-mouthed Toby jug. There was a thin, screwed-up slip of paper amongst the ruins, which I pocketed.

I had to think quickly. The kids were playing Dungeons & Dragons; only very, very stupidly. Uncle Kai was trying to explain the icosahedron to Mother, knowing full well that being forced to leave school at fourteen meant she had been marched to the cookery room to brainwash her in to believing the meaning to life lay in blind baking, not the number of sins revealed on a dice. There again, life's all just a role-playing game; just like the game played by the man named Bunny who lied about being a Spitfire pilot. The discussion in the lounge was getting sterner. Mother wasn't happy about something, so the noise bought me extra time. I hid the broken pieces in the kitchen bin inside the cupboard, and decided if I didn't say anything then I might be gone before anybody noticed the missing jug. But they would know somebody had hidden the evidence, wouldn't they?

Before I had time to think further, my aunt came through to the kitchen. "Come and have a look at the garden, Natasha," she said. "My son-in-law cut the grass."

We stepped outside and it was clearly freshly mown. "How nice," I said, remarking to myself how small and sloped the back garden was. Then my aunt added, "He's a lazy so-and-so," in an unpleasant tone, as if she had nagged him to complete the task.

We went inside, and that was when I made my biggest mistake. I decided to tell my aunt of the breakage. I said, "It was on the top here, I think. But I never spotted it. The next thing I knew was that it was on the floor. I hope it wasn't valuable."

But it was. Oh yes. She and Uncle Kai discussed its rarity and value. How much was it worth? Hard to say. I thought about offering to replace it. "I could buy you a new blue vase," I said. "One that's got a bit of gold on, too." Meanwhile Mother was yelling at the children, who were now running around in the hall. The house really was so much smaller than I thought it looked like from the outside. A sort of Tardis in reverse.

"Can't it be glued back together again?" No of course it couldn't. What a stupid suggestion. This incident really shouldn't have happened. How careless of me. I should be made to feel guilty about this for a long time, maybe even for the rest of my life. At every family occasion from now on, it will be discussed, brought out on show in place of the broken jug. The ex Toby Jug.

Still my aunt and Uncle Kai were discussing the Toby jug. They didn't seem to want me to try and replace it with another. They were more concerned about the history of it and its intrinsic worth. Damn the stupid Toby vase Jug thing, I thought, wishing I had just left it on the floor and not been so honest. Although my aunt had seen me retrieve it from the bin, so was aware I was considering concealing my accident.

What a to-do. I escaped for a while to the downstairs loo. It was stuffed full of toilet paper, and despite tugging bloody-mindedly on the make-shift rope chain, I failed to flush. My lipstick was smudged, and I had never tasted that Chilean red. They could keep it. If the Toby jug was so valuable, why hadn't they looked after it better? Still, it started well enough. When I hoped nobody was looking, I tipped a selection of tiny sandwich triangles and spongey-looking snacks into a carrier bag for eating on the nightmare coach trip back home.

When I told this story years later to a group of people in a pub, somebody said, "Anybody seen that German film about a man who broke a jug?" Everybody muttered no, they hadn't, so he proceeded to say, "The judge is trying a case to determine who broke the jug. Long before the evidence becomes conclusive against the suspects, it becomes apparent that the blustering, bullying and naive village judge is the guilty one."

I replied, "What a boring film that sounds."

"No more boring than your story, Natasha." I had obviously upset him.

Somebody else in the group jumped in and said, "Anybody see the girl with the broken jug fountain in Catherine Park in St. Petersburg?"

"No," was the unanimous reply. "Do you have a photo?"

He slid images across the screen of his smartphone, and came across a photograph.

"That is so beautiful," I felt I had to say. "What was the story behind this broken jug? Do tell!"

Some more Googling, with the following result: the milk maid is from the fable by La Fontaine, crying over the broken jug of milk. She personifies the futility of human dreams. The statue was ordered by Alexander I in the early 19th century. Alexander Pushkin was inspired by this fountain to write a romantic poem, "The girl with the pitcher":

"In dropping the urn of water, the maiden broke it on the cliff.

The maiden sits sadly, holding the useless shattered pottery.
A miracle! The water keeps flowing from the broken urn;
Above the eternal stream the maiden sits eternally sad."

As with all stories, there seemed to be various interpretations of this tale surrounding the girl with the spilt milk. One overriding message seemed to be that one shouldn't count one's chickens before they hatch. That old bugbear of rags to riches and back again.

"Most importantly," said the guy who had introduced me to La Fontaine and Pushkin, "did your relatives ever forgive you? You seemed to think you would be forever tainted by breaking their precious antique?"

"I hardly ever visited them. You know. Christenings, weddings and funerals. But for some reason, we were all invited to their house miles from everywhere." I slid the images on my smartphone across to reveal the house, to show them.

"And the Toby jug. What was it like?" Again, when they had all looked at the house image, I found a photo I had saved which looked vaguely like the jug I had broken.

"My aunt and Uncle Kai were muttering between them how they had discovered the item in an antique shop in the Lake District. How it couldn't be replaced. What puzzled me was they must have been using it in the kitchen, as it was with all the crockery. If it had been that valuable, it should have been covered by their house and contents insurance, and maybe locked away in a cabinet."

"Are you absolutely sure it hadn't already been broken? You said it didn't make a noise when it hit the floor? You mentioned a Chilean red? Were you already a little tipsy?"

Somebody else said, "You seemed to want to reveal your crime once your aunt had sniped about her son-in-law being a lazy so-and-so? Were you scared she would go mad at you if she tracked you down before you confessed? She sounds an ogre."

"Couldn't you have just said you were sorry. That you instinctively cleared it up. That you would pay the cost of its worth. And leave it at that?"

"But," said somebody else, "it appears her aunt and Uncle Kai weren't content to just leave it at that. They were grieving over something that had sentimental value to them."

"Then why not just glue the goddamned thing back together, stick it in a cabinet, and forget the whole issue."

"Does your aunt actually like you, Natasha?" By now, I was confused by all these questions. As Monty Python pontificated, "Nobody expects the Spanish Inquisition."

"I don't know what they think of me. All I can say is since that day I have only ever sent cards, and yes, I do worry that when my aunt and Uncle Kai die, my cousins might chase me for compensation."

"Ethan Frome," said a stranger who must have entered the pub only a short time earlier, but had eavesdropped enough to join in with the broken conversation. "I assume you are familiar with Edith Wharton's novel of that name?"

I shook my head, and said, "Is the plot about a broken vase?"

"A red glass pickle-dish," said the stranger. "The cat got the blame, but the breaker of the pickle-dish confessed to leaving the dish in a vulnerable place. People tend to keep their precious things hidden away or up on high shelves, and only ever bring them out for special occasions, to impress or to pretty up a table."

"Despite the breakage," I ventured, "did the story have a happy ending?"

The stranger turned to leave the pub, but before he exited, he looked back over this shoulder, and said, "The owner is described carrying away the fragments as if she were transporting a dead body."

There was a collective pause before somebody said, "That is just dreadful. Simply dreadful."

"I know." I sighed, looking again at the photo of the fellow sad breaker of a jug. And it had all started well enough.

I wished throughout my life to feel something, everything, so complete; a memory piece. That one time I did, I never, ever wanted to feel that way again. My last innocent year. It was like being winded and not knowing if I'd ever be able to catch my breath again. I wondered if pneumonia did that to an old man's lungs before it cast him over to the other side. I thought about the sixty-year blip posited by an economist frustrated at the castigation of the so-called boomer generation. America had their baby boom earlier from 1946 to 1952 when the troops came home and the breeding programme began. For the UK it came later, peaking in 1964, before the birth pill was rolled out and smaller families became the norm. All those boomers would need to be looked after by the tax payer. But all they are is a blip. Analepsis and prolepsis: flashback and flashforward. The ministry of time. The war that never ends wars; the ridiculously overpriced wedding; the pilot that never was. The lies we keep on re-living.

As for that thin, screwed-up slip of paper I had pocketed? It must have been secreted — unbeknownst to my aunt and Uncle Kai — within the hollow handle of the Toby jug. I forgot about that for many months after the visit. Upon retrieving it and unravelling it, this was the faded message from the broken jug:

Warning: This item may have a paranormal attachment. We want you to be well aware of what you're purchasing prior to making your selection. We've seen things at the end of the garden, things that cannot be explained. One of the entities was caught on thermal imaging camera.

Then one day, dammit, I decided to get in touch with the son of the aunt and uncle who owned the broken vase.

"Now there's a funny thing," he said when I rang him and related the incident. "Actually, I do remember." My cousin chuckled, and said, "There was something very odd about it. After the row when you broke it..."

"I did not..."

"Alright, keep your hair on. As I was saying, things started to get very weird. Mum and Dad went back to the shop they had acquired it from, with the intention of asking if it was repairable. Only they couldn't find the shop, they got lost on the way home, and ended up with a flat tire to boot.

"Then when they returned home, opened the boot to find it, the vase was nowhere to be found. We searched the house, and I found it in the bin in the kitchen where you had hidden it when you broke..."

"I told you it wasn't my fault." I didn't mean to yell at him.

There was an awkward silence before I apologised for the outburst and let him finish his story.

"Right, where was I?" he said. "Ah yes, well when I took the pieces of broken vase out of the bin to show Mum and Dad, then they started having a go at me. Saying it was my fault the vase was broken, and I had allowed you to take the blame."

"So how come they took the vase to the shop to get it repaired?"

"Well, this is where it gets even more crazy," said my cousin. "Mum blamed Dad for forgetting the vase, and Dad said it was Mum who was making such a fuss about a silly old vase which created the wasted trip."

"But it was your dad who made the most fuss about the vase being valuable," I said.

"That's not all of it," said my cousin. "They then argued over who had bought it and why, as neither of them liked it, and that it very likely never even came from that antique shop in the Lake District, which no longer existed, and likely never did exist."

"Your dad has travelled all over with his work. Maybe it was something given as a gift, it got packed for the next move, and then just landed up with them when he retired."

"Things got stressful after that. I even had to take time off work for it. You see, I swore that I had wrapped up the pieces of that thing in newspaper and placed it in a box with other items to be taken to the tip. Then, a few weeks later, I opened a cupboard to clear out more of Mum and Dad's things, and lo and behold the vase was there intact."

"Could it have been one of a matching pair?"

"I thought that was possible. But as chance would have it, my old college was having a class reunion, so I thought I would take it along to see if anybody might be interested in taking it off my hands."

"Don't tell me something awful happened."

"Nobody died, thank goodness. But the marquee collapsed, and a number of my old classmates were falling out over whose fault it was. So the vase got forgotten. There was something I did manage to find out, though."

"It's haunted?"

"Not by a ghost but a mischievous god."

I laughed, and wished I hadn't because my cousin sounded really cheesed off this time, when he said, "Having been left to cope with two very sick parents and a vase that seems to have a life of its own, I tracked down an old friend of mine, who is now a professor of international literature. He told me that sometimes people invoked spirits of loved ones when they were fashioning potteries. He also mentioned a god called Anansi, who was a dab-hand at causing mischief just to spice people's lives up a bit."

That might explain how the vase seemingly managed to repair itself. Another explanation is that the god of mischief can transfer himself from one vessel to another; maybe he is a multi-faceted, multi-dimensional god, and I was onto something when I linked my fate with those others cursed by a broken vessel.

After my cousin ended the call, I remembered the note with the warning, which I had neglected to mention. Oh well, he seemed to have worked out for himself how a vase can be full of mischief.

Kevin stared dumbly at the vase, noting now the cracks — the stone scars of previous fractures networking their way around the body like veins. "A self-repairing vase," he mused. "That's one I haven't heard before."

"Just the thing for the clumsy florist," Hiram chuckled.

The younger man pictured the vase falling from its shelf, only to gather itself back together and rise from the floor, the way they showed things magically repairing in old sixties television shows by filming something falling then running the film backward. "My mother once had a vision for peel-away linoleum," he said. "No mopping. Just grab a corner and peel away the dirty layer."

Hiram nodded along as he pushed some hangers left and right on a standing rack, making room for the various dresses there. "Not a bad idea," he said. "Your mother sounds like she was quite the visionary."

"She was the queen of visionaries," Kevin scoffed. "Full of ideas. She could go on for hours about the most…" He cut himself short. She was barely in the ground… what, two hours? It was hard to tell with all the rain blocking out the sun. Time seemed to both race and drag at the same time in the shop.

"Well if she was a queen, I hope you attired her properly," Hiram said. "For her funeral dress, I mean." He turned, holding a plain brown dress by its hanger, a dress without form or design. "The right dress can… well, as the saying goes: Clothes make the woman."

DAGON'S DRESS

by J. Neira

Margo Galloway was sure of one thing. The crown of Prom Queen would soon rest on top of her head. In preparation for that, she'd spend one entire afternoon at her mother's favorite hair salon. It had been an excruciating process because, unlike her mother, Margo didn't enjoy having her hair pulled and rolled, or being stuck on a chair for hours.

Being self-assured, good looking, well connected and nice was a powerful combination. It kept both of Margo's feet planted on the ground and proved her as reliable to others. Her perfect auburn curls, now more immaculate than ever, and her bright smile attracted everyone's eyes whenever she walked into school grounds. She marched swinging her hips slightly and greeting each and every student that said 'hi' to her. What made her different was that she meant it, her smiles were sincere, and her replies were earnest.

It would surprise absolutely no one when she won the title of Prom Queen. There were more stakes in betting who would reign besides her as her benevolent Prom King. Ever since she'd enrolled in this school, bullying rates had plummeted to an all-time low as those that envied her found themselves needing to imitate her gentle behavior, and the rest simply followed suit, enchanted by her niceness.

That day, with the wind caressing her newly cut and styled bob and wearing the latest fashion on top of red soled heels, Margo walked into school with an impish grin on her face. "Good morning, Frank," she told the old custodian who was sweeping the floor around the entrance.

The man pulled back his headphones and pressed the pause button on his Walkman. "Morning, lil' miss." He nodded at her and grinned, showing Margo exactly where he was missing some teeth. Margo wasn't deterred by the sight.

"Looking good today."

"Thank you, Frank. You know how it is, only the very best for the very best," she replied, offering the man her best smile, a practiced gestured that no longer made her cheeks hurt. By now they were numb whenever she pulled the corners of her lips upwards.

"Can't waste much time chatting, miss. Congrats on your win, by the way."

"My, Frank," Margo cocked her head, letting her curls reframe her face to show a better angle. Out of habit, she blinked repeatedly, batting her eyelashes, "I haven't won." Yet, she thought.

"Yet," Frank added. He waved an index finger in the air, "it's just a matter of time, kiddo." He clicked his tongue as she shook his head. "It always is." There was a somber tone to his words, but Margo thought nothing of it. The man was old and had too much in his head for her to bother herself with what he might have meant.

She gave him one last comment about the day and went on with her day, making a mental note about possibly spending less time speaking with him. There was something about Frank that did give her 'the creeps', but maybe watching too many cheesy horror movies left the impression that school janitors kept terrible secrets and pasts that should never be uncovered. At the end of the day, Frank was a quirky old man who did his work and didn't bother anyone.

That, Margo could respect. The man knew his place, just like Margo knew hers.

Her first class was History. She sauntered into the classroom and bowed slightly, making an event out of her entrance and garnering a round of applause from her classmates. Margo giggled behind a perfectly manicured hand and told everyone 'Hi'. Most of the students gawked at her while returning her smile, but a trio of young women had their eyebrows raised at her.

Margo blew a raspberry at them and sat on the empty desk right beside them. The girl closest to her, Asian and tall, with round glasses sliding down her nose and rich pink blush on her cheekbones, handed her a notebook. "I won't make fun of you today, if only because you lent me your notes."

"How gracious of you, Ana," Margo quipped back. She bit the tip of one of her nails and felt her shoulders relax. Her eyes settled on the other two. "What about you?"

Monica and Stacy, twin sisters with opposite tastes in hairstyles and color palettes, rolled their eyes at her, with Stacy taking longer to return to her original expression. Monica, the one wearing her hair in locks, spoke. "Stacy can't talk because she wants, and I quote, 'to conserve her voice' for choir practice, and I decided I'm done with saying mean stuff. It'll give me wrinkles."

"Says who?" Ana inquired.

"Says I, right now." Monica drummed her fingers on the desk. "Besides, every time I dare to mention the smallest not positive thing about someone's outfit, Margo starts snapping her fingers like crazy."

"That psych unit convinced me to try some classical conditioning with you." Margo said. "Glad to see it worked."

"A bit too well," Monica whispered under her breath and crossed her arms. "Right?" she asked her sister, who spent a handful of seconds looking back at Monica absentmindedly before nodding. "What's up with you? Ugh, I'm not talking to you before choir practice, you're impossible."

Margo snapped her fingers and Monica screeched before glaring back her. She'd caught her off guard, as usual, and once again had showed the others just how much power Margo had over them. She had a certain aura about her that made even her closest friends do whatever she wanted. Luckily, Margo usually wanted nothing but good things.

Order and peace, mostly.

Their teacher entered the classroom, binders and books under his arm, but the contents of the lesson were something Margo had already gone over on her own and allowed her mind to drift off, thinking about poor Monica and Ana, the latter of whom couldn't stop making fun of the former. To think they used to be the meanest girls around before Margo had decided to set the record straight.

They were gorgeous and fashionable from head to toe, but their hearts hadn't shared that outer beauty. Monica had been known for her nasty comments and Ana for being the worst tattletale in the school. Nothing happened without Ana knowing about it and then telling every living being inside school grounds about it. That's how people came to know about Tammy's college aged boyfriend. Poor girl, she was too naive for her own good, thought Margo.

Stacy, for her part, let herself be dragged around by her sister and her friend. Margo's addition had done little for her individuality, but at least the twin spoke louder and seemed overall happier around Monica.

The teacher was in the middle of a tangent about modern Greek customs and comparing them to their ancient counterparts. Someone mentioned that belief in Greek and Roman gods was becoming more common as of late, especially around young people interested in the occult and alternate belief systems that were, in their opinion, more welcoming. Margo scoffed internally at that; she didn't appreciate neither the arcane nor shameless displays of heresy. Still, she took notes of a couple of comments the teacher made about myths and rituals that would surely appear in the next test.

After that and an endless Math class that failed to entertain Margo much, as she could already memorize complicated equations and rarely made use of calculators beyond her very own gray matter, it was time to head out for lunch. Yesterday, she'd made sure that her family's maid had prepared veggie wraps with little sauce. Just a dollop, enough to avoid the food feeling dry. She could easily eat the school's menu, but it rarely had anything that went well with her diet.

In any case, the lunch lady's special mush was as tasty as it was attractive to the eye, and Margo considered it material for an oil spill photo collection. The sport's team seemed to love it and the lunch lady was indeed incredibly friendly, so that was yet another opinion that Margo rightly kept to herself and herself alone. Ana and Monica saw a face when they saw the strange dish at the cafeteria. Stacy, instead, followed mindlessly, her gait slow and unbalanced.

Margo placed a hand on her shoulder as the group made their way to their empty table. "Hey, are you okay?" She led Stacy to the table closest to the tallest window in the cafeteria, one that no one else dared to sit at because everyone knew it belonged to Margo's group. "Have you had anything to drink?" Margo offered her own scented cold tea filled thermos to Stacy.

Monica blew away a curl of hair that kept falling over her face. "Let her be, she didn't get any sleep because of her oh so dear choir. Gosh, out of all the thing to get excited for…" She shut her mouth after a quick snap of Margo's fingers.

"C'mon, Stacy. Sit here while I get you a soda." Margo made her way to the only vending machine in the cafeteria that had diet drinks. She pushed the buttons gently after inserting a big enough bill and chose a cherry flavored one. With the metal cylinder in hand, she turned. She froze.

Margo Galloway was a nice girl, things rarely shocked her enough to cause her to lose her cool. But there was one recent thing that made Margo uneasy whenever her eyes saw it. Saw her. The new student, Tara, was walking… No, creeping towards her table. Slowly, her form slouched and closed off to the rest of the world and face hidden by curtains of perfectly straight, dull brown hair covered in grease and in dire need of brushing.

Tara was the newest newcomer of the school's alumni, and she could only be described with words that Margo refused to say out loud. Brown and dusty tones for her clothes, nothing that would have made her stand out from a crowd except for her entire demeanor. Shy would fall short of what Tara appeared to be like. She seemed to be one breeze away from falling to the ground either from anemia, as concluded from her pale skin and dark eye bags, or excessive sweating.

The girl was always dripping.

It was, in Margo's most sincere and deepest opinion, utterly disgusting. But neither Tara nor anyone else deserved to be regarded with anything other than respect, so Margo took a deep breath and returned to her table, fixating on the image of Tara's back. The closer she got, the easier it was for her to hear what Tara was saying to her friends.

"So," Tara spoke in that raspy and painful voice of hers, "will you vote for me, please?"

That hit Margo like a slap across her face. Was Tara, of all people, really competing against her? Margo's first instinct was to laugh. She reigned that impulse in and forced her winning smile to appear. It almost faltered when her friends replied with quick nods and nothing else. The lack of a cutting comment from Monica weirded Margo out.

Margo's presence made Tara jump. For a quick moment, they looked into each other's eyes before Tara practically ran away from the scene of what Margo considered a crime. To Margo's dismay, she noticed Tara approaching other tables in the cafeteria with the same request. She turned to her friends, who finally snapped back to reality.

"Did someone spit on your food or what?" Monica asked as she blinked repeatedly. The gesture made it seem as if she'd just awoken from a dream. Ana and Stacy were in a similar state. Margo dismissed the comment, offered Stacy the cherry soda can and sat down to eat her own lunch. Out of the two veggie wraps inside her designer bag, she could only eat one.

It wouldn't be until a bit later, right before her Art class, that she felt normal again. In control. She tailed Tara for a short while, knowing that this was the only class they shared and that it would be her only chance of speaking to her without too many interruptions.

Tara was pulling a notebook out of her locker when Margo suddenly appeared by her side. "Hey!" she greeted, once more managing to scare the new student. "Oh, you look as if you've seen a ghost," she joked, pushing back the idea that Tara always looked pale and sickly. Margo quickly scanned their surroundings and exhaled after making sure that there wasn't anyone else close to them. She didn't let Tara speak before continuing. "So, I saw that you were going around lunch, talking to some people."

Tara whimpered and hugged her notebook. Right then and there, Margo caught sight of something strange. The fear in Tara's trembling lips and shaking shoulders didn't reach her big, shiny eyes. She blinked and whatever she'd seen disappeared. Tara spoke. "I guess… So what?"

Margo understood the defensiveness and shifted her weight from one foot to the other, letting her own posture relax to appear less threatening to Tara. "Oh, it's nothing. Just… You want to be Prom queen? That's unexpected, but fun! All these years I've run for the position uncontested; this might change things around."

The other just nodded.

It made Margo nervous. She rarely found herself having to force a conversation forwards. "But maybe it isn't the greatest idea ever, you know?" Her hand swung from side to side. "Some guys around here might not like seeing someone running against me and you're so new to the school. I'd hate if someone bullied you in my name." Margo raised her palms in Tara's direction. "But let me know if someone does ASAP. I'm super anti-bullying and will do my best to protect you from any nasty people."

Then, it was time for her smile. Toothy and white, perfectly straight. Margo grinned at the other young woman.

Tara said nothing.

"Uh…" One corner of Margo's mouth faltered. "It's what I do. No one gets called a freak under my watch. So how about you stop running around alone and join my campaign? It'll get you in everyone's good side in a blink. What do you say?"

At that, Tara did reply. A short and curt "nah," and her unblinking big stare. After that, she left, leaving Margo alone and stunned. The bell rang and time passed, and Margo remained there until someone ran past her and she, for the first time in years, was late for class.

To her dismay, things didn't get better the following days. The unrelenting efforts that Tara made to talk with other students and run away whenever Margo came within six feet of her would have been impressive for Margo if they didn't make her uncomfortable. Why was the new girl so fixated on stealing her rightful crown? After all she'd done for the school, after all she worked to achieve order and peace. Tara was someone to be reckoned with and Margo didn't like that one bit.

To make matters worse, even trips to the mall were not Tara-free. While out getting ice cream, Margo swore she saw the dripping girl slouch her way into a n old store called Goods & Services, only one of the o's had fallen out of Goods. But when Margo squinted to make sure, Tara had already vanished inside, and no way was Margo following her in there. She shook her head and went about her hunt for ice cream.

"We could make posters about her," Ana offered one afternoon after class as the twins drove them to the nearest ice cream parlor. "Some that says she eats her own boogers or something."

"She sure looks like she does," Monica added with a full body shudder.

"No, no, no, and no. Absolutely not." Margo glared at her friends as a warm feeling filled her chest. Their intentions were sweet, even if their methods were not. "No one is going to vote for her anyway, there's no need of making the girl have a bad time both before and after Prom once she loses." Because Tara would lose, she had to. "I'd be surprised if she gets one vote. Like, she's new and has no friends, why would she be Prom queen? Not that there's anything wrong with her but she doesn't represent the school."

"She's not so bad either," Stacy added. It was rare to hear more than a handful of words coming out of her mouth ever since that choir practice.

Her twin snickered. "Not so bad? She's been sneaking around like a creep."

Margo's fingers twitched. That comment would have deemed one snap from them, but she just couldn't do it. Tara had been going around, whispering right into other student's ears, including to the entire football team the other day, saying God knows what… The feeling of dread inside of Margo increased alongside her pity. The lengths that Tara went through just to ensure that she was considered as a valid candidate did garner an ounce of Margo's sympathy.

She'd been like that, once.

Maybe she should check her own privilege and give the girl a chance.

And then, one day before Prom, Tara cornered her.

"Will you vote for me?"

She blinked, having forgotten how to breathe. Margo failed to contain her uncomfortable laugh. "Excuse me?"

The weird girl marched away, not repeating her question. She didn't need to; Margo had heard her loud and clear. That had been bold, and Margo respected boldness. To give credit where credit was due, that audacity deserved a reward by itself. As such, when Margo, decked in her best dress and still with that perfect hair that had kept its shape, stood in front the ballot box with a piece of paper in one hand and a pen in the other…

She wrote Tara's name and pushed the piece of paper inside the box as fast as she could, fleeing from the feeling of regret. The deed was done, at the very least Tara would have one vote and it would be enough to make the girl feel welcomed. One vote would suffice to show others that someone deemed her valuable. It would include her in the rightful order of things and her state as a pariah would finally be a thing of the past.

Margo Galloway was a merciful young woman. A kind one, a logical one.

It was dark inside the auditorium, and the strobe lights that danced all around the place gave the room an unearthly ambiance. Bodies danced, voices screamed, and drinks pushed down throats that weren't old enough to legally taste them. It was barbaric and yet, another cog perfectly placed in the imperfect engine of high school. When she'd first entered through the auditorium's double doors, people had been chanting her name and someone had pushed a red plastic cup between her hands. The beverage had been passed along to another person, because Margo refused to get drunk in public.

She had to be ready to accept her crown and give her queen speech, after all.

She danced with her friends, twirling her long, mauve strapless dress and waving her arms, covered in white opera gloves, at the rhythm of the music. She was in the middle of a dance routine with Monica when the music stopped. The MC, an acne riddled young man that thought that wearing a cap backwards was still cool, cleared his throat right into the stage's microphone.

"The votes are in! We've got a king and queen!"

The students roared, cups flew, and someone threw a shoe up in the air. It was an ugly shoe in any case, so Margo didn't feel sorry for the person who would have to go all Cinderella over the missing slipper. A second roar rumbled through the dark auditorium when the school's quarterback was revealed to be the students' choice for Prom king.

Adequate enough. It would do, Margo thought. The MC brought up a second piece of paper after discarding the one with the quarterback's name and started to speak. "And our prom queen is, by unanimous vote with no other competition this beautiful night, is…" Margo preemptively smiled and then…

"Tara!"

She froze. Her mind was playing tricks, it must have been doing that. Unanimous. No competition. But it wasn't a trick. Her classmates and friends where clapping energetically and whistling, all with their backs turned to Margo. Not one set of eyes considered her as the crowd went wild, wilder… A figure slid through the noisy crowd and made its way onto the stage. The lifeless dress, mundane hair, uncovered face and clammy, sweaty hands made Margo want to puke for a moment. The dress had no shape, akin to a brown potato sack on top of a pair of beige sandals with no heel. Not one drop of makeup painted Tara's face, but her skin was so wet that Margo couldn't blame her for that, specifically.

She was still looking at Tara when the new girl looked back at her. At that moment, it finally made sense. How could it not? All the bad feelings washed away, leaving Margo empty and lost, yet strangely comfortable.

The silence was broken by Tara's raspy voice. No words came from those wide lips, only meaningless sounds and gurgles. Momentarily, Margo was reminded of a fish out of the water, grasping in the air for something it could breathe in. As quick as the image went, it left. Tara's vocalizations continued, becoming deeper and more complicated the longer she screeched into the microphone.

Margo felt something pull on the corners of her mouth. She started to grin not out of convenience but out of contentment. She was happy, she was laughing with Tara, not at her. No one was. Her hands went up and hung in the air.

"Thank you," Tara finally said, enunciating the words carefully, "for this." She pointed at the crown on her head with her clammy hands.

Then, Margo began to clap. Everyone else followed suit, mesmerized by their queen, going wild once more. The crow clapped until Tara left the stage and scurried away. Something broke then, and the party resumed as if nothing out of the ordinary had happened at all. Dazed and tired of the noise, Margo decided to put some distance between the chaos and herself. She made her way to the interior of the school, entering a much calmer hallway as she took a deep breath. Crossing the doorway, she crashed into someone else.

"Oh, sorry, Tara," Margo quickly apologized, suddenly much calmer now that the other girl was in her field of view. "Didn't see you come this way too. You caused quite a stir back there."

At the very back of Margo's mind, she couldn't help but compare her much more expensive and elaborate dress to Tara's simpler attire. Each girl appeared to have come from opposite ends of a fairy tale, with Tara being the pauper to Margo's princess. It should have bothered her, and being bothered by that should have bothered her too, because she fought against those urges daily. Instead, she thought of nothing beyond how charming the situation was.

"Congrats on being Prom queen." Margo lolled her head to the side, honestly brimming from her words with a force she couldn't contain. It was as if she couldn't feel anything else. "Enjoy that crown. You deserve it." She did, didn't she?

Tara gestured to the old dress she wore. "I got this at Goods & Services," she rasped. "He told me this was a gift from Dagon, who my people worship. My people... the refugees from Innsmouth. He's a human god, but he cares for everyone who worships him, even if they are only half-human, like me. This dress helped me win."

Margo laughed. She didn't mean anything bad by it. She was just confused by all those strange words Tara had just told her. It sounded like a confession, but who was she to judge?

Tara glared.

Margo laughed. What a charming queen the school had now. She laughed some more, hiding her mouth behind one of her gloved hands. Tara kept glaring with her too big, shiny eyes.

What a charming queen indeed.

"Hold on," Kevin said dazedly. "Isn't that a Lovecraft story?"

Hiram tilted his head quizzically. "Lovecraft? Don't think I know him. Some kind of writer?"

Kevin blinked. "You haven't heard of H.P. Lovecraft? He wrote, like, some of the most influential horror stories ever."

"Which ones?" Hiram seemed genuinely interested, taking a memo pad and stubby pencil from his shirt pocket, poised to take notes.

"Well, there was… There was…" Kevin struggled to recall the library shelf of his mother's bedroom. She was a voracious reader, consuming mysteries and horror stories. There was a whole bookshelf just of the scary stuff, with sets from King and Koontz and Barker. In his mind's eye he could see a stack of paperback reprints by Poe and Lovecraft, but he couldn't recall any of the titles. "There were… too many to mention. You should Google it."

"Google… it…" Hiram repeated slowly, writing the words down and disappearing the pad and pencil back into the pocket of his gray work shirt. "I'll do that." He then replaced the dress on the rack next to a ridiculously wide pair of britches with a pair of suspenders already clipped to their waistband. "Hmm," he mused. "Forgotten I'd had these. Don't think they'd fit you, but you might be surprised."

Kevin sensed the shop keeper was launching into another tale as the flip phone on the counter began once more buzzing like a hornet trapped inside a window pane.

Gods and Services: New Location

DEMI-GOD OF SUSPENSION

Jonah Jones

As he was strolling along Lupine Street in Pawtucket, Allie Gittfinger became aware that his diet was having considerable effect. His corduroy trousers, corduroy being significant, had slipped off his hips. The belt was below the lessened bulge of his belly and had become slackened to the point when it was ineffectual. Holding his trousers up with one hand, he looked around the crowded street to discover the nearest shop had apparently seen his dilemma and proffered a solution. Amongst the bric-a-brac, shirt collars and cravats, he had spotted a pair of braces in the window.

"Ah," Hiram Priest, the shopkeeper replied to his request. "Braces. You'd be from Britain, I'm assuming."

"Yes. Wandsworth."

"Here we call them suspenders. Makes more sense if you think about it. In a few days' time I shall be calling them bretel."

"Whatever you say. I'll take the pair in the window," Allie said, trying not to sound over-keen for the sake of keeping the price down.

"They're still a bit stained," Hiram admitted as he took them down from the silver display torso. "The last owner had a bit of an accident."

He stretched them and allowed them to spring back. "Still plenty of give. You'll feel right as rain in these. They're from the Old Country, too."

"I don't suppose you have any new ones."

"You don't suppose correctly."

"Very well – how much?"

Hiram smiled a smile that had spelled doom to many a customer. "No charge."

There was a pause as Allie tried to gauge that expression and take on board the fact that the suspenders were free.

"Seeing as they're stained," Hiram added to mollify any caution on his client's part.

Either he was going to be forced to make the rest of his journey one-handed or accept the offered article. Allie tested their elasticity and made a snap decision. "I'll take them. Is there anywhere I can put them on?"

The shopkeeper smiled that puckish smile again, then turned to look away. "Don't worry, there won't be any more customers today."

The trousers were so slack that Allie was able to pull the back around far enough to attach the braces to the buttons and then the two straps to the front. Still voluminous enough to accommodate his pre-diet belly, the trousers were flapping about but at least staying in place.

Allie turned to discover that Hiram had been replaced by a bishop of the Orthodox Church, ornately dressed in gold, green and white robes, his mitre plastered with jewels, accompanied by a bare-headed man swinging an incense burner. There was the gurgle-pop sound of a spatial shift, and the shop had moved on with its owner, bishop and censer wielder but Allie still wasn't alone. A dapper little man about three foot tall, who was wearing Hiram's smile, a cerise satin-lined dark cloak, side-striped trousers that fitted him and a top hat was dancing a poop-deck jig in front of him, a smile beneath his pencil moustache as he sang

> Here I come, the dancing one
> To take your hand and lead you on
> To give you half a chance
> For you to say yea or nay
> And sashay to the dance.

The diminutive character ended his soft-shoe routine with a flourish of his silver-headed cane, a shuffle of his feet and lift of his hat.

"Good day," he said with an extravagant bow. "Allow me to introduce myself. I am Hookatrice."

"Good day," was the best response Allie could muster as he looked around for the others who seemed to have evaporated with the incense smoke.

Anticipating the question, the pint-sized man explained "They were here for the services. I'm here for the gods."

Hookatrice tapped his cane three times on the paving slabs, causing them to shift and glide as if they were floating on an icy ocean.

Allie looked around for some reference to normality but found nothing that made sense. Any signs of civilisation were gone, and he was up to his ankles in the mud of a forest.

"Where's this?"

"Nipmuck."

"What are you? What do you want?"

"I am the Demi-god of Suspension."

"Suspension of what?

"Some would say disbelief, but I'll leave you to decide, and as for wanting, it's more the other way around. I am able to grant wishes."

"Are you like a genie?"

The short wyrdman scowled, causing the top hat to tip over his eyes. "How dare you! I'm a demi-god - not some flibbertigibbet of a slave with an outrageous accent and covered with lamp-black."

"So, Mister Demi-god, what can you do for me?"

"I can grant you half a wish."

"Half a wish is as much use as half a ping-pong ball."

"Demi-god – demi-wish. Those are the rules."

Once he had adjusted to demi-gods being less than half the height he'd expected, having been force-fed Hollywood's versions of superhumankind, Allie didn't spend too much time considering the wish. He just needed a good starter. "I wish for a million pounds."

Hookatrice waved his arms around for a touch of theatrics as much as anything. "Only do the currency of the place I'm in," he said.

There was then one of those pauses they put into games shows to wind you up and then,

and then again

THUMP!

A large bulging heavy-duty canvas bag landed on Allie's feet. After a wince of pain, he opened up the leather straps to reveal a heap of American paper money inside. He took a few bills out and saw the problem. They'd all been torn in half.

He looked askance at the demi-god and the demi-god returned the look, similarly askance.

"Half a wish," Allie said in explanation to himself.

"Indeed."

There was a pause during which Aloysius Gittfinger looked at the bag-full of half bills. Cursed with that name, he'd always considered that he was unlucky and a half. He'd never resolved the conundrum of cause and effect. Was he unlucky because of the name or was he given the name because he was born unlucky? Before him was the proof of the way his luck seemed to run. "I don't suppose they all match up."

"According to the way these things work, they will do, but you'll have to spend a bit of time sticking them all together."

Calculating that the mechanics would take him a month of Christmases, he had a better idea. "I wish for a two million pounds' – I mean dollars' worth – of gold. Un-marked gold."

Hookatrice nodded in appreciation of Allie's quick wit, summoned up his powers, closed his eyes, executed a twiddle of the arms, a stamp of a foot and after the pause of expectation

WHACK!

When Allie came to, his ears were zinging, his head hurt, and he had trouble breathing. Something large and heavy was resting on his stomach as he lay on the ground. He looked down to see that it was a decent-sized nugget of pure gold, glistering in the sunshine filtering through the trees.

"It's about four hundred ounces, give or take," Hookatrice assured him. "You should get about a million for that at today's prices. Not that I'm anything of an expert, you understand. I leave the financials to the gnomes - grubby little characters that they are."

Allie shook his head to clear his vision, then inspected the nugget. "Where did it come from?" he asked.

"The important point is not its origin but its destination. Id Est – the top of your cranium from a great height."

"Eh?"

"It bounced off your bonce. Concussion is nine points of the law."

Over the next few days, Allie was to learn by experience that it wasn't as easy to sell that amount of gold. The more he tried, the more paranoia gripped him. Dealers were sharky and shady, they might be ganging up on him like some cartel, they might be telling the tax creeps, they might be telling the criminals. He was getting nightmares. He'd never had nightmares before. Everyone in the streets was a potential robber. For a brief respite, he placed the nugget and the folding money in a deposit box in BankBoston. At least it would be safe there and he would in turn be safe on the streets.

"It's useless if I can't sell it," Allie said in disgust.

"It's very pretty," Hookatrice replied.

"What use is that?"

The demi-god shrugged. There was no pleasing some. He therefore changed tack. "Why did you want to sell it?"

"Money. I want money."

"And what use is money?"

"I can buy things with it."

"Why not simply wish for those things?" Hookatrice began prancing around, doing the shuffle and stomp, while counting off the advantages on his fingers. "No fluctuations in gold prices, no negotiating with dodgy dealers, no wondering what the Japanese are going to do tomorrow, or even what they did yesterday…complicated security systems…insurance…

You, me and the waves on the sea
Nothing but free.

Allie's eyes followed the gambolling demi-god as his brain thought that one through. The point had been made cogently.

"I wish for," he began, bringing the other to a one-legged stand-still in anticipation. There was another pause as he wondered for what he should wish. "I wish for a luxury yacht – two luxury yachts."

Hookatrice did the waving of the arms routine, there was a very distant

WHOOSH, SPLASH

but nothing apparently happened.

"So?" Allie asked.

"We are currently fifty miles from the sea, give or take. Did you want the yacht here, in the middle of a forest?"

"Ah yes." Another point was taken. "Where is it?"

"Boston."

"Okay - I wish to travel to Boston."

An arms wave, a horribly quick and vomit-inducing relocation and they arrived at Constitution Wharf, with Allie's gorge rising rapidly as he contemplated using the nearest part of the marina as a receptacle.

"I named it for you," Hookatrice said.

Allie looked along the line of luxury yachts until he found the one in question, "4U" inscribed across its luxurious stern.

Not funny. He hated text-speak even when his stomach wasn't jigging around the place.

"I'll be changing that," he told his benefactor.

"That'll be interesting, seeing as I've already registered it."

"You haven't had time."

"Time is just stuff. Like gold, like yachts. It's manipulable."

They got on board, had a look around until Allie realised there was something missing. "Does it have a crew?"

"You didn't wish for one."

"I wish for two crews."

The sound of heavy sea-booted feet approached along the pontoon until the crew arrived at the berth.

They were every sort of human being he might have imagined from some fantasy or sci-fi film, some of them several in one.

"Is this it?"

"They are the original motley crew. I thought you'd

appreciate some historical frame of reference."

Allie looked them up and down a second time. Some of them didn't even appear to have achieved the status of human and every one of them gave off an odour of neglect. Centuries' worth.

"I don't," he replied.

Having been instructed to head for the Med by their land-lubbing captain, they set off with a yo-ho-ho and a packet of Quells. Half an hour out and Allie felt just as well about the Quells. Two hours out and he was shovelling them down his neck like a stoker on a collier. Six hours away from land and the quells ran out.

Groaning whilst throwing up over the side, he managed to say, "I wanted to go to Saint Moritz and mix with millionaire birds in bikinis."

"How?"

"In my yacht."

"Did you mean Saint Tropez? Moritz is mountains. Birds in bikinis only après ski."

"By the sea?"

"Tropez yes, Moritz no."

Allie contemplated the prospect of all that sea going up, down and side by side, before getting to tangle with the millionaire set.

"In that case, I wish for two Lear Jets."

Pause.

WHOOSH – nothing.

Bleary-eyed, Allie looked at Hookatrice who responded to the tacit question.

"Figure it out. Seeing your condition, I'll give you a clue; Lear Jets don't float."

"They're on dry land fifty miles away?"

"Something like that."

"Would you be able to get me there without the sick bit?"

"Yes and no. Your gastrics are out of my jurisdiction."

# # #

After he'd cleared his stomach in the men's room of Logan Airport, Allie emerged to appraise his latest wish.

Standing in front of the Lear Jet at Logan Airport, Captain Bartholomew was a smart-looking reliably middle-aged male pilot in well-ironed dark blue uniform, topped by a hat with incomprehensible golden livery and a shiny peak. To his side was a stewardess with clothing short at the bottom and low at the top, leaving Allie's imagination searching for employment elsewhere.

Gauging his reaction, Hookatrice waved his arms, the stewardess gained fifty pounds, forty years and a dress from throat to ankles, suggestive as a potato sack. Although the scarlet lipstick remained the same, distraction was no longer an issue. The captain and she led them onto the aircraft where she introduced herself as Ludmilla Krauss with a faintly German accent and a canapé or two as she settled him down into his seat.

"Where are the parachutes?" he asked her.

"We do not have parachutes," she informed him with a toothy, lipstick fringed smile.

"Well, I want one," Allie said.

She raised an eyebrow at him, turned to Hookatrice and raised the other one, at which he did the conjure-it-out-of-thin-air routine, producing one which Frau Krauss placed under Allie's seat without batting an eyelid under the raised eyebrows. Apart from awkward customers, she was evidently used to the idea of things materialising at a demi-god's whim.

"Sir will be safe now," she purred, like a mother cat to a kitten.

"If everyone's ready," Captain Bartholemew intoned through the speakers, "we will begin taxiing."

"Strapping oneself in," Ludmilla suggested firmly, and Allie complied like a well-behaved child. Once she was satisfied that he was buckled in, she followed suit, leaving Hookatrice to hover gently in the background.

The Lear Jet accelerated and took off smoothly enough, rising quickly up and over the harbor dotted with the little islands and boats with white wakes weaving amongst them. Allie thanked goodness he wasn't on one of them, as the plane curved round and then set out over the open ocean.

The stewardess unbuckled herself and mobilised her eyebrows again. "Would Sir care for some champagne?"

"Sir certainly would."

She returned from the galley with a bottle of Moët et Chandon and a glass, set on a silver tray. Expertly she unwired and removed the cork with a slight thump and a hiss, to pour him a glassful.

He took a sip, found it brut enough to his liking, finished the glass and handed it back for a refill.

After the second glass, he burped.

"Everything must return to its resting state," Hookatrice intoned sagely.

Allie nodded in agreement and belched again.

The demi-god picked up his top hat, placed it upon his head, took his cane and tapped it three times on the table.

"You're not the only client I have on my books. The emporium is currently just off the Damstraat."

"The what?"

"In Amsterdam. Not far from the Cannabis Museum."

Hookatrice started to fade away. "Don't bother trying to find it," he said with that Mona Lisa smile. "It won't be there for you." Then he was gone, followed by the last glint of his teeth.

Allie felt strangely disappointed. He'd got used to having a demi-god around the place. He thought further about it. They say that you should associate with your slightly betters to become slightly better, and he realised that he had indeed become a more complete person for being close to a demi-god. He'd developed a greater sense of his own potential, if nothing else.

However, we should all learn to count our blessings and as he closed his eyes, Allie did exactly that. In a deposit box in BankBoston, he had a large lump of gold and a decent amount of folding money – which admittedly required the use of a great deal of sticky tape and elbow grease – but aside from all that, he was rich and was about to tangle with the even richer. He dreamed of possibilities as the Atlantic passed serenely beneath him. Marriage? No. Expensive and exotic mistresses? Possibly. Simply swimming in gold or perhaps caviar would suffice in the short term.

He gloated for a while, then called for more dream-inspired canapés with caviar. Response came there none, so he got up and walked to the back of the plane to find no one there. He walked to the front and found the cockpit was equally deserted. Either they had gone to Amsterdam with Hookatrice, or maybe simply evaporated. Not having the least idea of what he was looking at, he watched the dials on the various meters and weighed up the two obvious plans of action. Attempt to fly this thing and then land it or use the parachute. The Lear Jet forced the issue by starting to point its nose downwards. In a remarkably short time, Allie put it on, noted where the pulling handle was located, opened the door of the now vertical aeroplane and jumped, grateful for his foresight in asking for a parachute.

He was naturally a calm person, so when he pulled the cord to discover only half a parachute above him, he calmly looked for the spare and pulled that to discover there was only half of that, too. Two halves were not making up what he needed as a whole.

Of course, he should have asked for two but then might have ended up in the same position, given that he already had two demi-chutes fluttering above him, failing to do the job of one good one.

Without becoming hysterical, but at the top of his voice, he wished for a double-sized parachute; but the wish-granter was occupied elsewhere with a woman whose elastic had broken in a crowded accessibility lift in the Rijksmuseum.

Meanwhile, the Earth, for they had reached the lumpy bits of Europe, continued to hurtle towards him.

The bishop and his sidekick were also falling, but less quickly due to their large robes, now filled with air so that they resembled a pair of gilded Fabergé eggs as they glided down.

The goods might have been failing but services were being restored.

A lesser mortal would have panicked but Allie had been

touched by the gods – well, one god - all right, one demi-god, however the encounter had gifted him with, if not superpowers, then at least slightly superior human powers. The floating bishop had inspired him. Maybe he was no longer as unlucky as his name might suggest. Swiftly he took off his trousers, knotted each trouser leg, held them over his head, allowing the air to fill the rest of his voluminous pantaloons – corduroy, remember, therefore windproof – and floated gracefully down to a soft landing upon an Alpine meadow amongst the edelweiss, holding the suspenders as parachute cords.

Once he'd recovered his composure and re-trousered himself for the sake of modesty, he watched the air-filled men of the jewelled cloth, jingling as they rolled down the slope, their cassocks bouncing over the tussocks until they disappeared from sight. Perhaps they were Polish, he mused, then turned to discover aforementioned demi-god standing next to him on the flowery meadow, shuffling some smuttily illustrated playing cards, the top one of which he showed to Allie: The Knave of Diamonds in a very knavish pose.

"It's not far from the Red-Light District, too. The GAS Emporium, I mean."

"So, what now?" Allie asked.

"Now that they've done their job, I retrieve the suspenders, you go your way, and I go mine."

Allie scanned the mountainous landscape. It was going to be a long walk back to civilisation. Especially with oversized trousers and nothing to hold them up.

While he continued to shuffle the intriguing cards, Hookatrice read Allie's thoughts – another trick demigods have. Half the time, at least.

"Enjoy what you've gained and what you've learned. Don't be greedy. Use that nugget in smaller, less attention-grabbing pieces, buy yourself some trousers that fit and consider changing your name for one less unlucky. Arbuthnot Groole, perhaps?"

With a grin so wide it showed off his back molars, the short-changer of wyrd undid the magically and otherwise tainted suspenders, stretched them and allowed them to snap back, similarly snapping his smile from broad to broader as Allie's trousers fell to the sward.

"Everything must return to its resting state," he repeated solemnly before wrapping them around his top hat and dancing down the slope towards Kuala Lumpa, the next location of the Gods and Services Emporium, singing as he went:

Watch you the Trickster Man,
Barley and mow
Dance with the Hookatrice
Wherever he go.

"If at first you don't succeed," Hiram quoted, "skydiving probably isn't for you." He proffered the suspenders to Kevin with a wink. "Sure I couldn't tempt you? I can let you have them for… shall we say, half off?"

"A semi-price for a demi-god?" Kevin replied blandly.

"Semi… Say, that's pretty good," Hiram chuckled. "I may just use that."

Kevin shuffled, wishing he'd found shelter in a gas station or even a bus stop. The longer the old man talked about gods walking the earth, the more Kevin started to think he really believed such things.

"A skeptic, I see," Hiram said.

"What? I didn't say anything."

"That look says it all." Hiram shrugged. "It's all right. I get it all the time. Doesn't bother me. Mind you, some of the merchandise might react negatively toward it. I'd avoid the bookshelf in the back, if I were you."

"Because of all the gods."

Hiram smirked. "Because of some of the gods," he said. "You don't think they all just hang around the store waiting to be called into service, do you? Most of them are out there," he waved his arm in grand presentation. "Just waiting for their avatar to be taken in exchange for an offering. They have things to do, you know. Places to go. Other gods to chat up."

TWELVE STEP PROGRAM OF THE GODS

Bil Richardson

"OK, let's call the meeting to order. We have a new member tonight. Would you stand and introduce yourself?"

A thin, dark figure got to its feet. "I'm Anubis," the dog-headed creature yipped. "It's been five thousand years since I've been worshiped."

"Welcome Anubis," the others in the church basement intoned.

There was a foot-high dais in the front of the room. A woman stood on it. Dozens of breasts swayed under her loose-fitting shirt. There was a lectern in the middle of the stage, but she avoided it. "We've got a pretty big group tonight. I don't know if that's a good thing or a bad thing."

A polite laugh rippled through the room.

"I guess most of you know me but for those who don't, I'm Diana, Ephesian mother goddess. It's my turn to direct the meeting but we're all equals here."

"None of you are my equal," an old, red-haired man grumbled from the front row. "I am the God of Gods."

"Not anymore, Zeus." A muscular, blonde man in the back called. "Now the average joe couldn't pick you out of a lineup."

Hercules was sitting beside his father and shot to his feet. "Thor, just because you're getting some traction in popular culture doesn't mean you're a god anymore. They've turned you into a cartoon character. It's embarrassing."

"Yeah, and you'd kill for the kind of heat I'm getting," Thor smirked. He motioned toward Zeus. "I don't know why you keep defending this guy. You're just a bastard he abandoned. You should be harder on him than anyone."

A blue woman three seats from Thor hissed at him. Her fangs and many, waving arms made her menacing even when she wasn't trying to be. "Well, I don't see your father here," Kali growled. "I guess Odin thinks he's too good to attend a meeting."

Thor looked at the floor and mumbled. "Not everyone is ready to face their situation."

The goddess of destruction hissed again. "So, he's in denial?"

"No, I think that's Anubis." Loki deadpanned.

Diana cut in, trying to stop the direction the conversation was going. "First Loki, that was lame, even for you. Second, we have a rule. No picking on the new guy."

The god of mischief looked petulant. But that was normal.

Diana stepped down from the little dais. "Look, I know all of us need to let off some steam, but none of this is really helping. We're in the same boat. No one else knows what it's like to be raised up as a god one day and completely forgotten the next. So, let's support each other and stop this petty bickering."

"What about Loki?" Thor said. "Being petty is kind of his thing."

Diana pointed an admonishing finger at the thunder god. "You two need to leave your sibling rivalry at the door. This is supposed to be a safe space for everyone."

Thor rolled his eyes. "Whatever."

Diana scanned the rest of the room. "Who here wants to share something real, and not just posture or divert?"

A hand went up in the back. A man with red skin and horns stood. "I'm Satan. It's been—"

"Whoa," Zeus interrupted. "You aren't supposed to be here. Didn't you see the sign out front. This is for forgotten gods only.

"Look, I know there's still some who worship me. But just a few hundred years ago I was on top. No one doubted my existence. I was feared. There were covens everywhere. But now most people think I'm just a fairy tale. They don't believe in me as the personification of evil or the source of it. They think they're the reason for all the bad thing they do to each other."

"Yeah, but the Christians are keeping you alive. You're all they talk about."

He shrugged, accepting it. "Granted. But that's not the same as being worshipped. In the Middle Ages I was everywhere."

"I wish I had your problems," Hela, the underworld goddess grumbled. "I used to be where you are, but now I'm just a punchline. Hela good." She frowned. "What's that even mean?"

"Ah, I don't think that's exactly…" Anubis started to say but trailed off.

Satan put his hands up in a calming gesture. "All that is exactly why I'm here." He scanned the room. "With all due respect, I don't want to end up like you. I want to stop the bleeding before it's too late. I thought since you've been there, that you could give me some advice."

"Get yourself a videogame," Kali suggested. "You need the kids to believe in you and that's all they do these days."

"Or a movie deal," Thor added. Someone threw a coffee cup at him. He batted the Styrofoam away. "Alright, who did that? Was it you, Hercules?"

His bearded nemesis feigned innocence and the thunder god scowled at him. Zeus stood up and turned to Satan. "Look, there are things that are out of your control. A Jesus comes along and knocks you off the front page. Things like that. But there are also things you can control. You can't be complacent. Tactics that worked in the dark ages don't work anymore. You have to innovate. And most of all, stay in the game. You can't assume they'll keep believing just because they did in the past."

There was a murmur of ascent. Heads nodded. Satan pulled out a tablet and started taking notes. "OK. That's good stuff. But can you give me any specific ideas?"

"What about those plagues?" Kali said eagerly. "Those were huge. That's all anybody was talking about for centuries."

Satan seemed embarrassed. "That was actually Yahweh. I got a lot of the credit, but it was all him. Punishment for sins and such."

"What about sacrificing children? That was in the papers as recently as the 80s."

"Humans did that," Satan explained. "I don't know what made them think it was something I wanted."

"War?"

"People again. But usually in the name of God, or just wanting what someone else has."

"Well, what exactly have you done?"

Satan beamed. "I'm big in politics. Those people will sell their souls for almost nothing."

"So, you were responsible for Trump?"

Satan shook his head. "I wish. But Trump only worships Trump, so that was all him."

"Then how have you remained the dominant god of darkness for five thousand years?"

"The Bible mostly. If it wasn't for Christians keeping belief in me alive, I'd be nothing. I owe them a lot."

"Can you convert them?"

"I've been trying. I've got them preaching politics from the pulpit. Turning the other cheek and loving thy brother are totally on the way out. But I haven't been able to get them to take that last step and actually worship me."

"What about getting on Fox News. They'll know exactly how to convince their audience to believe anything."

"Rupert Murdock's whole family sold their souls to me decades ago, so I might be able to make that happen."

"Well, if you're trying to turn Christians, you've got to get on Fox. These days, they believe it more than the Bible."

Satan continued taking notes. "This is all good stuff. Anything else?"

"Do you have a Facebook page?" Loki asked.

Cthulhu waved this off with a tentacle. "Facebook is over. You gotta be on TikTok."

Satan looked up. "Tik what?"

"It's a Chinese brainwashing site," Kali answered. "But you'll have to learn to do the floss or, better yet, come up with your own dance."

"What kind of dance?"

Diana shrugged. "It doesn't matter. Just make sure it's funny. You can get a million followers overnight."

"A million. Really?"

"Yeah, people spend hours on it every day," the mother goddess continued. "Make a splash there and you'll be back on top in no time."

Satan saved the notes on his tablet. "Wow, you have all been so helpful. How can I ever repay you?"

"I could use a few retweets," Zeus said.

"And follow me on Insta," Loki added. "Our brands have a lot of overlap."

Satan checked his Rolex. "This has been great everyone. But I've got a meeting with some guy named Q in DC. We're eating at a pizza parlor that he says has human sacrifices in the basement."

"That guy's followers will believe anything too," Kali said. "They're perfect for you."

Satan waved as he headed for the door. "I can't wait to get started on this." He raised his fists triumphantly. "I'm back, baby."

When he was gone, the group turned to Diana. She looked at the clock and gestured to a table off to the side. "That's all the time we've got this week. There's still some cinnamon rolls left. Be sure to finish them off. I don't want to take any home."

Hercules gestured toward her chest with his coffee cup. "We're out of cream. Can you give me a few squirts?"

Diana folded her arms over her many breasts. "You gotta know you can't make those jokes anymore. You wanna get metooed on top of everything else."

Kevin stepped away from the counter and the annoying flip-phone that was angling decidedly toward him as the persistent vibrations made it dance across the plate glass. "You make the gods sound... well... human."

The older man chuffed. "Can you think of anything more frightening than a human imbued with divine semipotence?"

"Semi..."

"Not quite omnipotence," Hiram said. "All the gods have a weakness or three. A foible, a quirk, something. But that just makes them more fearsome. Their power and their weakness, together." He pushed his spectacles up the bridge of his nose. "It's a pretty volatile combination, don't you think?"

Kevin mulled over the idea, slightly aware that he was giving serious thought to the concept of gods as people. "Power and weakness," he repeated. "Yeah, I guess that makes us wee mortals mere pawns and victims of the gods' choices."

"Oh, who said they have a choice?" Hiram replied. He lifted a bolt of old tattered fabric from a bucket and made a show of inspecting it for moth holes. "There are, after all, higher powers they answer to. Gods over gods, you might say. Yes, gods over gods."

THE UNIVERSAL THREAD

Lauren Stoker

These damned mortals! They just weren't getting it.

Every time she set up a lifeline, weaving with painstaking care the warp and woof of time and action, they screwed it up and a thread got dropped or sneaked in where it wasn't intended.

She threw her hands up in disgust.

After centuries of mostly thankless work, Flo and her two sisters had at last received special dispensation from the Big Guy on the mountain to relocate to Manhattan. The world didn't center on Greece any more, they told Him, in case He hadn't noticed. And it was about time those guys upstairs practiced a kinder and gentler version of godding. Just because someone didn't put out for you whenever you wanted didn't mean Flo and her sisters should be forced to weave nasty things into the brave ones' lives, messing up their destinies and those of their children.

Plus, there was a whole new world out west that they could oversee on His behalf. He might be content lolling about for all eternity up among the clouds, swilling his ouzo and horndogging the females, but they wanted to travel, get out and about, try different cheeses. There was more to food, surely, than feta and olives. It would be great feedback for the Big Man, they'd finally convinced him. And New York made such a nice change from hot, dusty hillsides with way too many goats.

Of course, they'd foreseen that their defection would throw Him into a gigantic pout and there would be the usual inconvenient consequences. But it was so good to get away and see the world a bit, they'd forgiven Him when He changed them into dogs. "It's only temporary," He'd grinned. What was it with Him and that shape-changing business? For eons, they'd been His faithful dogsbodies without that imposition.

The "temporary" part meant that when they left their apartment, they had to be walked on leashes, which required getting chummy with the neighbors, as well as some inventive planning. It did give them a different perspective on things, like the tastelessness of purple, rhinestone collars. It was also gratifying to be picked up after, for a change. Thankfully, inside they could just be their regular, immortal selves and bodies.

Right now, in winter, the city's cold kept them in, swathed in shawls. Even so, they enjoyed the clamor and stimulation of city life, its craziness and creativity, and bringing order out of the chaos. Their warehouse loft on the Lower East Side gave them an eagle's-eye view of the goings-on below. From the street far beneath them, Flo heard the impatient honking of cars—Christmas shoppers mired in traffic and dying to get home and put their feet up.

Up here, out of the melee, the snow drifting calmly past the windows lent a sparkle of interest to things. You didn't see that back home, unless you were one of the big shots up the bloody mountain.

And they discovered they quite liked the hard-boiled New Yorkers. They had spunk. Little by little, they found themselves moving away from simply weaving what they saw in people's destinies, to nudging and pulling the threads here and there, just a bit, to affect a brighter future. Sandals on the ground, living among the mortals, instead of viewing them from on high from a considerable distance, made such a difference in empathy. Oh yes, those mortals could be maddening, but it was so satisfying when they became . . . less so. And happier.

Moving here and adjusting to the times, she and her sisters had ditched the unwieldy Greek names for ones more suitable to their seeming age and location.

But some things just never changed, like human bull-headedness. They didn't call it a "stubborn streak" for nothing. No weaver, mortal or im-, could pick that streak apart.

Take this one—Howie Strong. The Fate could see his face so clearly in her mind. Well, she should do! Her sister, Lois, had pulled him up enough times in her scrying bowl, showing him off to her sisters. Secretly, Flo reckoned Lois had a bit of a crush on him. Strong like his name, handsome, and big as an ox, even for a linebacker, Howie had been headed for fame—the big leagues, maybe even the semi-finals. Hades, possibly the Super Bowl! But then he had to go and flunk out of high school. Thought it didn't matter that he could barely read and write. Well, the big-time coaches and recruiters set him straight on that, although too late to be picked up. Even their sponsors knew football wasn't merely a game played by hormonal hulks. It was a cerebral test of tactics, a war game. Something the big shot Olympians certainly understood.

Poor Howie had lost not only the battle, he'd lost the war. Now he'd probably be working at McDonalds. Maybe forever. Nice pension that would bring.

Drawing her bathrobe tighter, Flo shivered and frowned at the mess he'd made of her weaving, snagging up her loom, then cursed and ran her fingers through her frizzy grey hair.

"Damn! This is going to drive me to drink!" Flo hollered over her shoulder to her two sisters, "Speaking of which, any of that ouzo left Mr. Z sent us? My headache can't get much worse."

"Nah," said Lois. "We finished that, luv, right after The Great Loud Mouth got into office."

"You mean, 'Not-So-Great,'" Flo shot back. "Sometimes I do miss the old ways. What he needed was a strong thunderbolt to the backside."

"True. I think we messed up a bit on his warp," Addy said.

The other two snorted. "You think?" Flo said.

"Too much warp and woof all the way round on that one!" Lois caroled. "I wonder what we were drinking that day…"

This reminded Lois of her sister's need for strong drink. "You know, we've got some of that retsina left, Flo." She held up the bottle. "That'll put the hair of the dog on ya!"

Addy twittered, then yapped (in case neighbors should hear).

"Oh, har, har," Flo grumped. "If I must, I suppose. 'S like drinking fingernail polish remover. What were they thinking, capping good wine with paraffin?" Her sisters shrugged.

Lois poured Flo a glass and passed it to her. "So, what's so awful with Howie's weave?" she asked.

"Here, you take a look," Flo grumbled, hoisting the glass of retsina and making a face. Her right leg had quivered only a bit, longing to scratch behind her ear.

Addy and Lois hobbled over, slapping across the floor in fuzzy, pink Gorgon slippers, and peering through their bifocals to see what could be salvaged.

"Oh, don't be so downhearted, Flo." Lois studied the loom over Flo's shoulder, then took out her tape measurer and ran it down the length of the piece. "That's quite an attractive streak of green going through just there."

Flo peered down, frowning. "Where? Oh, yes! I see what you mean, Lois."

Mortals here tended far too much to see green as the color of submission, even cowardice. A wimpy, girlie color, or worse to some—"earthy-crunchy." Conservatives in this country were always curling their lips when they saw the spring green logos of clean energy companies or "tree-hugging, liberal," pro-environment groups. But Flo and her sisters knew green was the color of growth and resilience, of nurture and renewal. Global harmony, for Zeus' sake, and kindness, as well! Life sustaining, of all the hues it was the most important. Without it, spring could never happen.

She looked closer and admired how the strong, green thread wove determinedly in and out of its neighbors: red, ochre, brown, white, and indigo. The pattern was masculine and serene. Even allowing for the occasional hiccup of a dropped thread or gaping hole, each neighboring hue complimented its neighbor.

"Hmmmm. Yes," Addy agreed, pulling her scarf tighter. "Howie always has a way of making friends, doesn't he? And such a sweet family, too. Real close, all of them. Don't forget, he spearheaded that lovely community garden last summer. What a green thumb he has! Got a lot of gang-bangers off the streets and helping out. The story even got picked up by the evening news."

Lois barked a laugh. "That sure put a kink in those sleazy slumlords' plans to raze the neighborhood to build their condo high-rises for the yumpie rich."

"True." Flo nodded. "After the mayor's endorsement, those creeps just slunk away with their tails between their legs." She laid aside her shears.

Addy patted Flo's shoulder. "Much too soon to cut it, Flo. I'd keep going if I were you. See what happens, come spring."

Rubbing her cold, cramped hands together, Flo peered up at them. "So you don't think this is… he's… a total loss then?"

Addy and Lois shook their heads.

"Oh no, Flo! That's love, that is," said Addy, pointing to the green streak. "That's the universal thread."

"It's kind of weird to think of all these ancient deities moving on with their lives into the modern era," Kevin said. *Not to mention how weird it is to think of them existing for real in the first place,* he added mentally.

"Everything's just an extension of the function," Hiram said. "Travel faster. Grow faster. Communicate faster." Hiram nodded at the flip-phone that had once again fallen into a temporary silence.

"And the… what, the Fates, they're the only ones with real choices," Kevin replied. "I remember reading about them in high school. Spinning the threads of life, weaving them into a tapestry." He blanched as the memory of today's funeral came back to him.

"Cutting them short," Hiram finished sympathetically. His eyes locked with Kevin's, held them with the gravitas of eyes that had seen more than their fair share of tragedy; more than a single lifetime could account. "It can make one feel quite helpless, I know. Sadly, it's those who feel the most helpless who often end up tumbling through my door.

PHOBOS-IN-THE-BOX

Kay Hanifen

Panic thrummed through my heart, pushing me to run faster and faster. The street was empty, so I needed to get someplace with witnesses. Hopefully, that would be enough to scare them off. Bullies were cowards, and like all cowards, they would flee as soon as it looked like there would be consequences for their actions.

There. Up ahead was a shop that read "Goods and Services," though one of the o's had fallen, so it instead read "Gods and Services." I could make out the vague shadows of a person in the window. Hopefully, they wouldn't object to my intrusion.

I could hear Jonas and the others shouting after me, calling me the kinds of slurs that would get them detention if they were ever uttered in front of a teacher. Risking a glance over my shoulder, I saw they were dangerously close and picked up the pace. I was never much of a runner. Severe asthma and being overweight made running in gym uniquely unpleasant, but despite the feeling of my throat closing and my chest constricting, I moved faster than I'd ever run before. Adrenaline is a hell of a drug.

The bells clanged merrily as I stepped inside the shop. As I hoped, they didn't follow me inside. My breath came out in wheezes as I reached into my backpack for my inhaler.

It wasn't there.

Shit.

When frantically digging through the bag didn't work, I tipped it over, dumping the contents onto the floor. Papers, textbooks, pencils, my phone, and my lunchbox all came tumbling out. But still no inhaler.

Did Jonas manage to grab it in the initial assault? Did I drop it somehow? I never let that thing out of my reach. If it was gone, it meant I could die. Panic closed my throat even further.

This was it.

I was going to die on the floor of a random shop.

A face swam in front of my blurring vision, and I felt a hand on my shoulder. "Breathe," the owner of the face said. The grip was grounding, and fighting through the panic, I focused on inhaling and exhaling.

My lungs were slowly but surely opening, though the constricted feeling was replaced by a tickle in my throat. Like with most bad asthma attacks, I knew I would be coughing for the next couple hours.

"Thank you," I said, wiping the tears from my eyes. Asthma attacks always made me tear up, so people loved to tease me for "crying over a little bit of exercise" (fuck you very much for that Coach Swanson).

"Are you okay?" the shopkeeper asked as he handed me a tissue. At least, I think he was a he. Not that I'm judging, of course. It would be a bit hypocritical for me to judge someone for being gender nonconforming considering my whole deal. But it wasn't the reason why I'm still not sure who or what I saw. Because to be completely honest, I couldn't really tell you anything about him aside from the name on his nametag. Hiram Priest. Every time I try to picture him, it's like looking at a blurry photograph. I know what he said and what he did, but I just can't see him in my mind's eye.

Sniffling, I wiped my eyes. "Yeah. I think so." Blinking, I finally took in my surroundings. It looked like I was in an antique shop of some kind, one of those small businesses that was so stacked full of things that I would sometimes have to suck it in as I made my way through the aisles. These were some of my favorite places to wander whenever I had the chance. You just never know what kind of cool things you'll find. I met Hiram's eyes. "Thank you for helping me. As soon as the coast is clear, I'll be out of your hair."

He jerked his head to the window. "You were being chased by those hooligans outside." It wasn't a question, just a statement of fact.

I nodded. "They'll get bored. They always do."

"Well, until then, have a look around. Let me know if anything calls to you."

"Are you sure?" I asked, getting up. My knees still wobbled slightly underneath me.

He waved his hand. "Well, it's a shop, isn't it? The whole point is to sell you something."

"I don't have much money," I replied, shoving my things back into my backpack and straightening up.

He headed to the register at the front. "You're still welcome to look. Just don't take anything, please. The punishments for shoplifting can be much steeper than you could ever imagine."

"I wouldn't dream of it. My name's Kestrel, by the way."

He raised his eyebrows. "Interesting name."

I smiled. "Thanks, I picked it myself." Admittedly, this was testing the waters. If he was cool with me, then this place might be a good spot to hide out whenever Jonas decided that it was time for a beatdown.

He smiled. "An excellent choice. They may be somewhat small, but they're fierce predators."

A knot of tension in my chest began to loosen, and it wasn't just my breathing returning to normal. He was not going to judge me for who I was. Throat tickling, I coughed into my elbow as my eyes skimmed across the shelves. "I use she/they pronouns," I added quietly.

He hummed. "That's nice."

Now, that knot completely loosened, and I felt myself take the first truly free breath I had since Jonas and his cronies cornered me on the way out of school.

I wandered the shelves, my fingers occasionally running across fabric or the textured surfaces of ceramics. The place was a mess of items haphazardly thrown together. Loose jewelry sat beside teddy bears, which sat beside glassware. Everything looked ancient and valuable, but the price tags were oddly cheap.

"How come I've never seen you around before?" I asked as I held a staring contest with a Kewpie Doll.

"I'm new here," he replied smoothly. The layer of dust on some of the items for sale said otherwise.

My eyes wandered until they settled on a little box with a handle on the side. A music box? I approached slowly and picked it up, examining it further. The front depicted a man with a lion's head gazing backwards at a monster, his eyes on fire. Every other side depicted an image of terror, all in the style of ancient Greek pottery.

"It's a unique Jack-in-the-Box, isn't it?" Hiram said behind me, making me jump.

I fumbled with the box, nearly dropping it, but his reflexes were faster than gravity. He caught it midair. "Sorry, sorry!" I exclaimed.

He smiled and handed it back to me. "Don't worry about it. There's something about those little toys that always make me jumpy too. It's the anticipation of it, I think."

"Like a jump scare in a horror movie," I said, running my fingers around the edges. Slowly, I began to turn the handle, listening to the tinkling music playing.

Hiram caught my hand, stopping the song. "I'd prefer it if you didn't do that in my shop."

"Right. Sorry." I set it back on the shelf with the rest of the wares.

"Would you like it?"

I glanced over at my backpack. Mom had given me twenty bucks to keep there in case of an emergency. I didn't see a price tag on the box, but a lot of the items in the store looked expensive.

"How much is it?" I asked. I wasn't sure why I wanted this thing so badly. It was a toy for toddlers, but something about it drew me to it.

He picked up the box and studied it for a moment. "How much you got?"

I blinked. "Like, twenty dollars, I guess."

He stared at the box before nodding decisively. "Does ten sound fair?"

"Uh, sure." I fished the twenty out of my bag and handed it to him, shoving the box in my bag while he collected my change.

It was dark by the time I left the store, which didn't make much sense. I was chased in there while on my way home from school. There was no way I could have been there for over five hours, but the clock on my phone said that it was almost eight at night.

As I left the alley, I glanced over my shoulder. The shop was now dark. Gooseflesh prickled up and down my arms and I picked up my pace, speedwalking home.

"Keith, where have you been?" Mom demanded.

I swallowed back the urge to remind her that it was Kestrel now, not that she would listen.

She hadn't listened the past hundred times.

I had hoped that picking the name of a badass bird of prey would help ease my parents into the whole not-a-boy thing, but no luck. "Sorry, Mom. I just found this new antique shop, and I lost track of time exploring it." Technically, I wasn't lying. I just didn't tell her everything.

"Well, you missed dinner. It's in the fridge. Your dad wants to talk to you after you eat." With that, she turned on her heel and stalked off to the living room.

I swallowed, my mouth growing dry. When I first came out, Dad tried every troubled teen program and conversion therapy he could think of to drive the queer out of me. Nothing worked, of course, but that just made him more frustrated. And eventually, he took out enough of his frustrations on me to land me in the hospital. After the visit from the social worker, he stopped.

Everything.

We'd barely spoken three words to each other since that incident. What changed?

Suddenly nauseous, I decided to skip dinner and head straight to whatever fresh hell awaited me.

Dad was in his office nursing a glass of whiskey. Never a good sign. I knocked on the doorframe. "Mom said you wanted to talk to me?"

He gestured for me to sit down. "Come here."

I sat across from him at his desk, feeling like I was just called to the principal's office. The main difference, of course, being that my school principal had never put me in the hospital.

He had a pile of brochures in front of him, all advertising different boys' boarding schools and military academies.

Shit.

They were sending me away, throwing me to the to the mercy of teenage boys. I could barely survive public school here. How the fuck would I survive an all-boys' school when I'm not a boy? They were going to eat me alive.

Inside my bag, I heard two quick notes from the Jack-in-the-Box. Vaguely, I wondered what had jostled it.

"Keith, your mom and I have been talking. We think that there isn't anything else we can do for you here. You need discipline, and we clearly aren't equipped to give it to you."

I stood up, the chair clattering behind me as the more notes played inside my bag. "No, what I need is parents who love and accept me for who I am." Tears pushed against the limits of my eyes, threatening to spill over

"I'm doing this because I love you," he snapped. "If you keep going down this path, you're going to die."

"And if you force me to go to an all-boys school, you're going to be the one who killed me."

He slapped me hard enough for the tears to spill over. I brought a hand to my stinging nose and wiped it, my fingers coming away red. They curled into fists. I wanted to hit him back, but it would do me no good. So, instead, I turned and ran upstairs before he could grab me and inflict further damage.

Shutting the door behind me, I locked it and then braced a chair underneath the handle. With a stifled sob, I staggered to the closet and sat inside. He probably wouldn't bother me until the morning, but I was a wounded animal, and hid on instinct.

The box chimed again, and I lifted it from my backpack. Some of the blood from my fingers smeared on it, and my tears left wet splotches. Both absorbed into the box in seconds, which struck me as odd. The blood, at least, should have left a trace, but it was gone, as though I'd never touched it in the first place. The air shifted, becoming tense like the minutes before a thunderstorm.

As I studied the box, I felt the inexplicable urge to turn the handle. Most Jack-in-the-Boxes played "Pop Goes the Weasel" but not this one. The tune was old and haunting, one that invoked images of bloodlust and battles, massacres and monsters.

Something clicked in the box, and it opened. A face leapt out. Like the image in the front, it was leonine in appearance and fire blazed in its eyes. But that was where the resemblance ended.

A black ichor dribbled from its teeth, and its face—if you could call it that—looked to be more scar tissue than flesh. And it was huge, far too big to fit in that small box.

Shrieking, I dropped it and backed away, my lungs constricting my breath into wheezes.

Not now. I can't have an attack now.

"Keith!" Dad yelled, throwing the door open and sending the chair flying. The Jack-in-the-Box slowly turned to face him. It turned. All on its own. Dad blanched. "What the hell is that thing?"

Unable to take enough of a breath to speak, I just shook my head. I don't know.

A torso formed, and arms pulled free from it. The Jack-in-the-Box dragged itself towards him, its leering face still grinning maniacally.

"No! Get away from me!" Dad ordered, staggering backwards, but the monster didn't listen. Dad tripped and landed on his back, allowing for it to crawl its way up his chest and meet his eyes.

"See your worst fear made manifest," it said in another language. And yet, I could understand it as easily as I understood English. I didn't know why, and I had no interest in learning the answer to that mystery. The only reason I didn't run was that the monster was blocking the entrance.

And then Dad started screaming. He didn't stop as the monster shrank back into the box and Mom called an ambulance to get him help. They left me behind as they raced to the hospital.

It was just me and the monster in the box. "What are you?" I asked it. "What did you do to him?"

That night, I dreamt of wars in ancient Greece, of the terror of being caught up in the field of battle, bodies crashing against me like a ship on the rocks as we were surrounded and slaughtered.

And in the middle of it all was a monster with leonine features. He stood by his father's side and led the charge in terrorizing mortals on both sides of the conflict. A name echoed in my mind: Phobos, God of Terror.

When I woke, the box sat innocently beside me. I could have easily written off the whole night before as some strange dream, but when I checked my phone, I saw a message from Mom.

They're admitting him into the psych ward. Get yourself ready for school. I'll explain everything when I get home.

I wasn't sure if I should feel guilty or relieved over what happened to Dad. It was my fault, but after all the bullshit I suffered while dealing with him, it almost feels like justice.

There was someone else, though, in need of a dose of terror. Anything to get them to leave me alone. So, when I packed up my bag for the day (making sure to include my inhaler this time), I placed the box inside as well.

The school day passed as it always did. I kept my head down, never made eye contact with any of my fellow students and avoided answering any questions. That didn't stop Jonas and his merry band of idiots from following me as I walked home.

"Where do you think you're going, freak?" he asked.

It wasn't the most creative opener, but my heart nonetheless skipped a beat or two. "Home," I replied. "Like I do every day." The box in my bag chimed a note.

"What's that sound?" he asked, grabbing me by the backpack and unzipping it, digging inside like he owned it.

Finally, he pulled out the box. His lips curled into a cruel sneer. "This is a toy for toddlers. What the fuck is it doing in your bag?"

"It was supposed to be a gift for my nephew," I lied, snatching it back from him.

"Well, it's not anymore." He reached for it, but froze as I turned the handle, letting the unsettling music hang heavy in the air. He exchanged uneasy glances with his cronies.

The box clicked, and Phobos flew out. He latched onto Jonas with enough force to send him falling backwards to the ground. "See your worst fears made manifest. Give in to your terror."

Like Dad, Jonas then began to scream. His two cronies also cried out in terror, both turning on their heels and sprinting away. But Phobos was not far behind. With only his upper torso free, he dragged himself after them like a furious mermaid. I still don't know how he moved so quickly, but the other two boys were no match for him.

With his task completed, he folded himself back into the box, leaving me alone with three bullies lost to the terror of their own minds. Sticking the box in my backpack, I called an ambulance and left.

Jonas and his cronies were admitted into the same hospital as Dad, and like him, I never saw any of them again. Dad died of a stress induced heart attack soon after he was committed, and I never bothered to learn about Jonas's fate.

I still carry around the Jack-in-the-Box everywhere I go. A god, after all, needs believers and sacrifices to survive. Phobos may be the god of terror, but his companionship has become a comfort to me after all these years. He saved me from my worst bullies.

I remind myself of this fact every time I feed someone else's sanity to my god.

"Wait, so there's basically a… what, a serial killer out there? That you're responsible for?"

Hiram shrugged. There are several serial killers out there." He equivocated with his hands. "I may have played a role here and there with some of them. But responsibility is on the individual, wouldn't you agree? Just because I sell you a blade of Xipe Totec doesn't mean I make you commit ritual sacrifices with it."

Keven opened his mouth to argue, then jumped. His hand was resting on the glass counter and the flip-phone began vibrating again, somehow right next to where his hand had been resting.

"Why don't you get that," Hiram suggested. "It sounds like it may be important."

Tentatively, Kevin lifted the phone, then silenced it by flipping it open? "H-Hello?" he spoke.

The blood drained from his face and his hand began to tremble as he held the phone against his ear.

"I didn't leave…" he said. "Well not that early. But you were… Wait how is this…?" His breathing quickened as he leaned back against the counter to brace himself. "Of course. Yes, I… Hang on just a second."

Kevin cupped his hand over the phone. "How much for the phone?"

"The Eshu model flip-phone?" Hiram asked. "Eleven dollars and sixty-two cents."

Kevin hurriedly dug out his wallet and opened it. Inside were a ten and a single. He jammed his hand into his front pocket, turning it inside-out and uncovering two quarters, a dime and two pennies.

"Tax?" he asked.

"Never believed in it," said Hiram as he cradled the two wadded bills and the loose change in his overly-long hand. "Do you need a receipt?"

"No," Kevin said. "No, thank you." He was already walking toward the door. "What?" he said into the phone. "No, no, I was talking to the clerk. I was just checking out. No, Mama, I'm not spending beyond my means. I make good money, Mama, I'm allowed to buy a new phone if I want to."

The door closed behind him, the tinkling of the bell over it signaling his exit as he entered the bright sunset, the atmosphere washed clean after the downpour.

Hiram sorted the money into the cash drawer and rang up the sale. "Funny little chap," he said. "Most people want to at least know the terms of service before they enter a cell phone contract." He hummed absently to himself as he took a small cardboard tray of jewelry from behind the counter and began arranging the rings and pendants on the display tree.

GODSEND

Damascus Mincemeyer

The mid-August New Mexico evening was still warm when Daryll Carver pulled his Peterbilt into the tractor-trailer parking area of the Steel Wheel Roadhouse just off Highway 54. During daylight hours the place was an oasis for vacationers driving the endless sun-baked stretch between Santa Rosa and Alamogordo, a stopover for gas and grub and not much else, but after sunset the Steel Wheel became a haven for a harder crowd, bikers and long-haulers eager for cold drinks, hot women, and big trouble.

Thirty minutes inside and Carver sensed already it was his lucky night. He'd picked up a hitchhiker once south of San Jose, a cute little brunette with a moon tattoo on her wrist and tits that jiggled just right when his rig hit a rough patch of asphalt, some hippie-dippy New Age bimbo who'd talked about crystals and Chakras and astrology.

The stars were arranged in a certain way when you were born, she'd told him. And every so often the angle of the planets will align in a way that play off that arrangement and shower you with luck.

A transit, she'd called it, and that's what Carver knew was happening tonight; the second he walked in his favorite Judas Priest song, 'The Ripper', started blasting from the speakers, then he won a hundred bucks at the pool table. Better than any money, though, was meeting her.

Carver was on his second cheeseburger when he noticed the woman through the cigarette haze, perched at the opposite end of the counter and looking his way. She was twenty, twenty-five at a stretch, a platinum blonde goddess with a strappy white tank top glued to her torso and a pair of Daisy Dukes. She'd spent ten minutes not-so-demurely batting lashes before making an approach; up close she was more attractive than from afar, and when she slid onto the stool beside his, Carver noticed her dangling silver earrings and the crescent pendant wedged tantalizingly in her cleavage.

The roadhouse's music was raucous enough, the background chatter just loud enough, that Carver couldn't hear the blonde's name once she introduced herself; Serena, maybe, or Sabrina, but lot lizards weren't known for using their real names, and Carver's libido didn't care anyway. His only concern was that she looked clean; no telltale track marks or meth mouth. He'd screwed his fair share of gutter skanks during his tenure carting freight, and recognized this wasn't one of them. She was too fresh, too pretty, a college coed turning tricks to make ends meet, perhaps, or some small town hick looking for kicks in all the wrong places.

They sat side-by-side, flirting, before Serena or Sabrina or whoever she was eventually leaned over and whispered in a sultry dulcet, "Let's go somewhere…quiet."

She was let a seductive finger linger at her bosom, and Carver's heart fluttered. "I got a sleeper in my rig," he told her expectantly. "Can't get much quieter than that."

The semi-parking area was distant enough from the roadhouse that the Steel Wheel's neon scarcely sliced the gloom. Carver's Peterbilt was a two-door 389 Model, red and chrome and immaculately kept, with an extended-length hood, a thirteen-speed manual transmission and fully-loaded trailer. The interior cabin was functional, spacious, with every amenity: a SmartNav system, Bluetooth, satellite radio, WiFi and USB ports; there was a 78-inch length bed in the sleeper compartment partitioned behind the front seats with accommodations for shelving and a small TV, even a mini-fridge.

"Ain't much, but it's home," Carver boasted once he'd helped the blonde into the passenger's seat. For the first time trepidation showed; with the door closed, the cabin, roomy as it may be, was still confining, and her thumbs uneasily kneaded the small clutch in her lap.

"It's nice," she replied, still nervous. "Cozy."

From Carver's past experience the transition from flirty small talk to discussing the fee for blowjobs was often awkward. He attempted to put her at ease by showcasing the assortment of dashboard knick-knacks accumulated in his travels: a tiny ceramic Siamese cat from Florida, a spur from Idaho, a Packers button from Wisconsin.

"I like souvenirs," Carver assured her. "Spruces the place up."

"Suave and sentimental. Quite the catch." Serena-or-Sabrina motioned to a row of pictures above his head. "Who are they?"

Four Polaroids, each of a different young woman, were affixed to the sun visor. "Oh, those are my girls," Carver beamed like a proud parent.

"They're your daughters?"

"I said they're my girls, didn't I?" he snapped, then apologized. "Listen to me. Cranky ole' hermit that's forgotten his manners. Didn't mean nothin' by it."

There was a clumsy pause before Carver jerked a thumb towards the sleeper partition. "How 'bout a beer? Keep a few cold Millers in the fridge by my bunk. Don't tell anyone, though. The D.O.T. would not approve."

He gave a conspiratorial wink, and Serena-or-Sabrina's smile slowly returned. "It'll be our secret." She zigzagged a finger over her chest. "Cross my heart."

And hope to die, Carver added as he reached between the dividing curtains. The small Vipertek stun gun concealed on one of the bedside shelves fit snugly into his palm and was capable of delivering enough voltage to incapacitate someone three times his passenger's size. Without warning he flipped the device to crackling electric life, then thrust it towards the blonde.

He'd expected her to scream; they always did. What he hadn't anticipated was one quick hand blocking his forearm while the other punctured his throat with a hypodermic needle neatly plucked from within her clutch.

Sudden heat rushed up Carver's neck; he swore, battered the syringe aside, but his fingers lost their dexterity and the stun gun dropped harmlessly onto his thigh. He grew woozy, dizzy, confused. The fuck is this?

"Where's my sister?" the woman demanded.

"...What..." Carver's mind began to fog. "...What are you..."

She tore a photo from the sun visor. "This isn't your daughter and we both know it. Where is she? What did you do with her?"

The girl in the picture had rosy cherub cheeks and a pixie cut, a moon tattoo on the wrist: the hippie-dippy astrologer from...where was it?

"You took her," the woman continued. "Just like you took the others. Just like you were going to take me."

"...Fuck...you..." Carver slurred. "Fuckin' bitch."

The blonde retrieved his stun gun, and her glare then wasn't pretty or flirty or apprehensive, but aflame with purpose. "I know you, Daryll, who you are and what you do. I've seen it." She stroked her crescent pendant. "All this time you thought you were the hunter. But you never once considered you might be the prey."

Carver wasn't thinking anything then. His consciousness shriveled from whatever sleep she'd pumped into his veins; he tried resisting, but his limbs became leaden, his tongue felt swollen, and he slouched into his seat as the darkness devoured him.

# # #

Even as kids, Selene and Luna were polar opposites. Freckled and fair-haired, Selene was the classic overachiever, responsible and studious, concerned with schoolwork and books and getting into college. But Luna, wild little Luna, their mother's late June Moon Child, was the family's free spirit, a constant whirlwind of questions and curiosity. She'd loved anything that promised excitement—roller coasters and rock concerts, fast cars, good times and bad boys.

Despite their differences, the pair were close. Whenever some jerk inevitably broke Luna's too-trusting heart, it was Selene's shoulder she'd cry upon, and Selene admired her sister's devil-may-care brashness even if she never admitted it aloud. Still, they didn't always see eye to eye. Sometimes they fought. They'd been fighting that last time they'd seen each other, and Selene hadn't forgiven herself since.

It was just after Luna's birthday. She'd graduated high school a few weeks earlier and had talked all spring about road-tripping the length of the 101 from Seattle to L.A. She'd even saved enough cash from odd jobs to buy a second-hand Camry specifically for the journey.

"It'll be an adventure," she told Selene before starting out. "Just us and the open road. Masters of our own fate."

Selene was out of nursing school for the summer, and only agreed to accompany her sister to allay their parent's worry; they, like everyone, knew Luna's proclivity for wading into troubled waters and, ever the dutiful older sibling, Selene went along for the ride.

Those first few days were actually fun. The pair sang to the radio, posted silly Tik Tok videos, and hit every kitschy roadside attraction and taco stand they came upon; Luna even connived Selene into stopping at a tattoo parlor in Gold Beach in order to ink her left wrist with a blue moon.

They'd reached Northern California when Selene got food poisoning from a hole-in-the-wall crab shack in Klamath and spent a pained night curled over the toilet in a chintzy motel. The illness laid her up for two days, yet when Selene expressed interest in curtailing the trip, Luna stubbornly resisted the idea. The argument escalated, turned nasty, and Luna chose to spend the night sleeping alone in the Camry.

The next morning both she and the car were gone. A note was on the nightstand beside a wrinkled wad of cash.

Here's money for a bus ride home, Luna wrote. I'll text once I get to L.A. Promise. XOXO

Selene's calls were redirected to Luna's voice mail; direct messages went ignored. Still feeling miserable and without another option, she took Luna's monetary offering and hopped a Greyhound to Tacoma.

When Selene told her parents what happened they were upset, but Selene figured with space her sister would analyze the situation, see the messages and send a text. They'd share a laugh about how stupid and overblown the whole thing was, and soon Luna would return from her walkabout, no worse for the wear and ready for the next escapade.

The police call changed all that. July Fourth weekend, California state troopers discovered Luna's Camry abandoned on the shoulder near Ukiah; the transmission had gone out, and Luna was nowhere to be found.

A meager investigation provided nothing. No eyewitnesses or video surveillance to furnish any sort of timeline. After Selene recounted the circumstances of Luna's departure, a detective even suggested her sister had willingly disappeared.

"She'll turn up," the policeman said reassuringly. "You'll see."

A missing persons report was filed, but as days became weeks hope slowly faded. The constant stress put Selene's mother in the hospital with heart palpitations; her father, who hadn't drank since she was little, picked up the bottle again. Selene, though, busied herself with searching. She created a Facebook page devoted to locating Luna, and even traveled to Ukiah one weekend in a rented Sonata to post fliers and ask around. That was how she discovered the pendant.

It was a rainy Sunday afternoon. Selene spent a dismal morning trooping along every storefront, handing out the missing posters she'd printed; she was already hungry and tired and dreading the long drive home when she passed a novelty shop, small and squeezed between a hair salon and hardware store. The exterior was in bad shape: one of the O's had fallen from the awning, but the bespectacled fellow working inside was gracious enough to let Selene tape one of her fliers in the window. Just prior to leaving, she noticed the rain had started again.

"Fuck," she groaned, feeling embarrassed then that the owner heard her. Instead of getting insulted, though, he offered an understanding smile.

"Don't fret, miss. I'm sure its just a passing shower. Take a little time and look around. You never know, maybe you'll find something you can't live without."

Perusing the store's odds and ends proved disappointing. Everything was old, dusty, tarnished; Selene's mom loved antiques, much to her father's chagrin, and she shared his antipathy. To her, antiques were estate-sale cast-offs at best, worthless junk at worst.

Then the pendant caught her eye, half-hidden behind an old fur hat, its finely-crafted chain and silver crescent glinting in the store's dull lighting. Examining its ornate design more closely, Selene immediately thought of Luna. She'd love something like this.

The store vanished the instant Selene's fingers brushed the pendant. Suddenly the images she saw were no longer her own, but from somewhere else: a wide-open desert highway, a greasy man's cruel smile, a red-haired woman bound and bruised and pleading for her life; there was a caustic flare and the woman became a petite blonde, tied naked and bleeding inside a leather harness, then a pretty Latina hanging from a hook, then a screaming brunette. Pressure mounted in Selene's head with each successive scene; sounds overwhelmed her—a roaring engine, sadistic laughter, then the world turned to magma, bright and hot and flowing red.

Only the owner shaking her shoulder broke the spell. "Miss? Are you okay?"

Selene's eyes snapped open and she found herself back in the musty shop. Scarce seconds had passed, though it seemed so much longer. She dropped the pendant to the linoleum. "W-What...what just happened?"

The store owner cocked an eyebrow. "Just checking on you. You were so quiet I thought you'd left. Sure you're all right?"

Selene's forehead throbbed, but she said, "No, I'm fine. Really."

"I see you chose Diana."

"What?"

The store owner stooped to retrieve the pendant. "In antiquity a crescent moon represented Diana. Roman goddess of the hunt. Crossroads and underworlds, too, if memory serves. Once she was worshiped by millions, but thanks to ole' Marston she mainly sells funnybooks these days. Quite the comedown, you ask me. Fine piece of craftsmanship, however. You have excellent taste."

Selene's mind felt like an increasingly choppy sea, storm-tossed and spinning. Pulling the pendant from his hand, she searched for a price tag, but found none. "How much do you want for it?"

"Less than you may think," the owner replied. "Come on up to the counter."

Selene followed, but didn't recall much about the transaction. Her next clear memory was being in the Sonata, fogging the windows with each breath. Rain hammered the roof, but she scarcely noticed; all she heard were pained shrieks and desperate cries, echoing inside her head.

She had no idea how long she sat, but gradually the spinning stopped. The weather calmed. Night fell. The waxing moon rose, half-full and bright.

The pendant rested in her palm; when she finally secured it around her neck, the vision, the hallucination, whatever it was, replayed itself, in evermore extreme detail. Selene repressed the urge to scream, to rip the pendant off and throw it out the window, but she kept it on, kept her eyes clenched tight. To watch. To be sure. That she wasn't crazy. That she wasn't dreaming.

Selene saw each woman again, tormented, tortured, torn asunder. She felt their pain as her own, but fought the anguish, focused, studying the faces more clearly than before. Then she knew she'd been right. There were four women.

Four women. Three strangers.

And Luna.

# # #

Carver once heard scuba divers who ascended too quickly would sicken from the rapid decompression. The bends, it was called. That's how he felt as consciousness returned: in the bends, senses dull, mind groggy, joints aching. The cab's overhead lights glowed and when Carver finally rolled over he saw he lay on the sleeper compartment's mattress, wrists secured with duct tape behind his back.

"Good. You're awake," a nearby voice said, and it all came rushing back: playing pool, meeting the blonde, getting pricked with her needle. Ain't supposed to be like this, Carver seethed. I'm the Big Bad Wolf, goddamn it, not her.

Carver had met devious broads on the road before, trick-rollers eager to shake down unsuspecting johns, but he'd always knuckled them bloody and took what he wanted anyway. This bitch was different; she'd come prepared. There was something else about her that unsettled Carver, something he couldn't quite understand:

She'd known his name.

"Can you hear me, Daryll?" the woman asked. She hunched beside him, Carver's stun gun tight in her right fist.

"The fuck is this?" Carver spat, still dizzy, before thrashing against his crude restraints. "Let me go, bitch! You hear me? LET ME GO!"

His captor visibly suppressed a laugh. "Let. Me. Go. How many times have you ignored that plea, Daryll? From how many people?"

"Fuck you," Carver sneered. "The fuck you know me? I ain't never seen you before."

"No. But I've seen you. From your very beginning." Iciness froze the woman's gaze. "Daryll Lee Carver. Eight years old when you dismembered that stray tabby. Remember? You liked the way it yowled, the way it squirmed, the warm blood slicking your fingers. It's how you equaled pain with pleasure, so you kept doing it. Cats, dogs, anything you could get your hands on and your knife into. Your father caught you once, with a neighbor's rabbit, saw what you'd done and knocked you senseless. But the beating didn't curb your appetites. You started fantasizing about doing to a person what you'd done with the animals. Then fantasy wasn't enough."

The woman raised her free hand. One of the Polaroids from Carver's sun visor confronted him: the redhead. "She was twenty-eight. Mother of two. Trying to get her life back after years on heroin. She liked tin roof sundae ice cream and surfing and The Beatles," the woman flicked the photo at Carver and held up another, that willowy ash-haired Idaho girl. "She used to model as a teenager, but turned down a contract because she wanted to take care of horses. Her girlfriend had just proposed the week before, and she was so excited to be planning a wedding. And this one—" The third picture arose. "—was going to be the first in her family to finish college. She loved tennis, and hiking, and old Humphrey Bogart movies.

"Three lives, Daryll. Three people you used, desecrated, disposed of. You thought nobody cared, that nobody would find out, but you were wrong."

Carver shrank into the mattress, shaking his head. "T-This is some kinda trick. Ain't no way this shit's real. Ain't no way."

The woman continued like he hadn't spoken; she unfolded a piece of paper from her clutch, and there was the face of the hippie-dippy astrologer. MISSING, the paper read.

"This is Luna. She's nineteen. She loves candy corn and singing along to Billie Eilish and being fashionably late to every appointment." The woman's tone hardened. "You stole her. Violated her. Is she in pieces like the others? Where is she? WHERE?"

The woman tore open Carver's flannel shirt and jabbed the stun gun into his torso; the first screaming shock electrified his nerve endings and seized his muscles, but his captor kept jolting Carver again and again, relentlessly, shouting each time:

"WHAT DID YOU DO WITH MY SISTER?"

# # #

After leaving Ukiah, Selene journeyed farther south. It was a compulsion, just some irrational gut urge, but she followed it, if only to soothe her ever-mounting anxiety. She wasn't even sure where she was going or why until she spotted a diner in Los Gatos and felt compelled to stop.

"You're back," the waitress said once Selene settled into a booth. "Ever get your car fixed?"

Selene politely shook her head. "I'm sorry, you must be mixing me up with someone else. I've never even been to San Jose before today."

"You sure?" The waitress frowned. "Swear on my momma's grave it was you. Must've been your long-lost sister if it wasn't. One of those faces, I guess."

The comment startled Selene; sweat beaded her forehead, her hands shook. She showed the waitress one of Luna's missing posters. "Is this...is this who you're talking about?"

"Oh, that's her," the waitress confirmed. "Came in all upset a couple weeks back, said her car broke down and she'd been hitchhiking. Worked the manager into a tizzy by only ordering coffee for four hours. 'This ain't no rest stop, Missy,' he told her. They got into an argument and she stormed out. I felt for her, though. Our manager can be a real prick, and she was a sweetheart. Dramatic as hell, but sweet."

Outside, in her rental, Selene was more perplexed than ever. Luna was here, she marveled. Her mind erupted then: she saw her sister, red-faced and crying, exiting the diner at night, saw her walking alone along the highway's shoulder, saw an eighteen-wheeler stop and pick her up.

Then the vision was gone and Selene was driving again, west, into Nevada. The desert unfurled around her, beautiful, vast, empty, and she drove for hours without stopping, without food, without rest. At times it seemed she wasn't in command behind the wheel, as if someone else was steering the course.

She took a room at a motor court in Hawethorne and finally collapsed, exhausted, onto the bed. The nightmares started almost immediately, vivid, terrifying episodes, screams and blood and butchery; Luna wasn't in these; no, these were of the others, the women she'd first envisioned in the resale shop in Ukiah, only these experiences went deeper. She bore witness to their lives, where they were from, who they were.

Jeanne, the redhead, was a sometime prostitute and full-time addict in Tallahassee. She'd been at the tail of a week-long binge when she accepted a ride from a trucker, and they made idle conversation for half an hour before Jeanne realized they were traveling the wrong direction. Somewhere over the Georgia state line the truck driver pulled a taser, and two months later Jeanne's dismembered corpse would be scattered across seven states with none the wiser.

Margot was thirty-one, a dishwater blonde veterinarian outside Twin Falls who volunteered part-time at a horse ranch and made the error of falling asleep in the stable one afternoon. She was awakened sometime later by a man she mistakenly believed was there to transport two colic-stricken mares. Embarrassed, Margot apologized and followed the man to his truck. Eight weeks later her unidentified skull washed up on the shore of the Snake River.

Alessandra's family was El Salvadorian. She'd been a lot like Selene, bookish and bright and working her way through UW Madison. One chilly April night Alessandra joined some friends for a Girls Night Out pub crawl, but she drank too much, got separated from the others and quickly became lost. It was raining and the Uber she called was late, so when that cherry-red rig stopped for her, Alessandra was so happy to be warm and dry she overlooked the driver's peculiar behavior until it was too late.

Selene slipped into a pattern: she'd drive to parts unknown—Nevada, Arizona, New Mexico—letting that strange instinct guide her to a gas station or a truck stop for reasons she couldn't fathom; at night she dreamed, sometimes of Luna, sometimes of the women abducted before her, sometimes of their kidnapper and his depraved acts. Other dreams were of Selene herself, running through an unfamiliar forest, heart pounding, muscles ablaze with exertion, dodging trees and boulders and roots. Something fled ahead of her, shadowy and elusive, something she was intent on capturing.

Rounding a bend, Selene saw a woman standing in the woodland path, draped in a resplendent cloak and carrying a bow and quiver of golden arrows, wearing purple half-boots and a jeweled belt. Her flowing dark hair was gathered in a ribbon. Her skin glowed. Selene, suddenly fearful, skidded to a stop.

Hearken, the woman announced, and her voice sang unlike any other. Wondrous, clear, perfect: the voice of the Divine. You have offered supplications, and I bestow a gift in return.

The woman outstretched the bow, but Selene was too afraid to move. Instead, she asked, W-Who are you?

The woman's eyes gleamed. Pray to me and by the full moon you shall find your prey.

Again, she extended the bow. Selene hesitated, yet this time reached out. After waking, it became so clear: the purpose, the visions, the driving instinct. She understood what she was doing, what must be done.

Five nights later Selene parked the Sonata in the far corner of the Steel Wheel Roadhouse's lot. It was a rowdy joint, loud with music and alight in devilish neon. The day had been blistering, and for an hour she rested with the windows rolled down, studying every passing vehicle.

At eight-forty a bright red rig chugged into the semi-parking area. Selene slouched in her seat, watched the truck and waited. After a few minutes the driver climbed from the cab, wiry, with narrow cheekbones and a mean, loping gait; he passed Selene's rental to the roadhouse without paying the slightest heed.

A Ziploc bag in the Sonata's console contained a small glass bottle and syringe. The previous day Selene stopped south of Albuquerque, and walking into the Duke City Urgent Care knew exactly what she was after. Midazolam was a common pre-surgery anesthetic; a single dose would induce sleepiness in a two-hundred pound man, and filling the needle she pondered her ability to thieve it undetected, as if she'd been shielded by some protective cosmic hand.

Selene slipped the capped syringe, a small switchblade and some duct tape within her sequin-covered clutch. She'd bought both purse and knife in Albuquerque along with a tank top, some cut-offs and fuck-me pumps; the outfit felt oppressively clingy in the heat, but did wolves complain about sheep's clothing if it brought them closer to their quarry?

A full moon lit the sky when Selene exited the car. The walk across the lot was agonizingly long; part of her desired to turn and run, though she knew that wasn't an option, not after coming so far.

Bikers on the sidewalk whistled at her approach, but Selene brushed off the advances and pushed her way to the roadhouse's entrance. At the door uncertainty gripped her and the itch to flee returned. Instead she grasped the pendant, closed her eyes and murmured a prayer before steadying herself and going inside.

# # #

Carver writhed on the mattress. "STOP!" he screamed as the woman prodded the stun gun into him. "Your sister's here, all right? SHE'S HERE!"

The woman straddled him; her left hand gripped his throat, the right poised the Vipertek over his bare chest. Raw red whelps kissed Carver's midsection; spittle oozed from his mouth; his fingers twitched involuntarily.

"You're lying," Serena-or-Sabrina snarled, but Carver feverishly shook his head.

"I'm not," he rasped. "She's...she's in the trailer."

The woman paused, and Carver could practically read her thoughts: Should I believe him or not? Finally she eased back. "Show me."

"Undo my hands."

The woman hesitated, then nodded. "Try anything and you're dead."

She cautiously set the stun gun aside, pulled a folding knife from the clutch, then rolled Carver face-down and sawed through the duct tape. Once finished, his captor goaded him to the passenger's door. "Outside. Now."

Carver was still lethargic from the injection, but the arid evening air invigorated his senses. His truck was sandwiched between two other rigs, and the narrow space was dark; fifty yards away the Steel Wheel rumbled with boisterous energy. Carver reasoned he was too far for anyone to see him, but if he made a break for it...

And how am I gonna distract this bitch long enough for that?

He contemplated it, then announced, "You know, your sister begged for her life."

Serena, Sabrina, whoever, shoved him. "Shut up."

Carver smirked in the gloom. Got her. "You never see who someone really is until you put the screws to 'em," he continued. "Some are Fighters who'll claw at you every chance. Some are Bargainers. They'll promise anything to go free. Money. Drugs. Sex. Anything. Your sister, though, she was a Beggar."

Another shove. "I fucking said shut up."

"Beggars try to play your sympathies. 'Oh, please don't hurt me. I'm too young to die. I love kittens. I've got a family.' Like I give two shits." He leered at his captor. "What are you, I wonder? I bet you're a Fighter."

The woman pushed Carver hard upside the trailer's cargo doors and edged the knife against his Carotid artery, yet her voice sputtered when she spoke: "S-Shut your mouth and open the truck."

She's spooked good, Carver thought happily. When the woman's grip slackened, he unfastened the latch securing the right-side door and swung it wide, exposing shipping crates stacked to the trailer's roof. Carver pointed to a thin aperture between two towering rows, barely wide enough for someone to squeeze through.

"Back there," he revealed. "Your sister's back there."

The woman didn't budge. "You first," she ordered. "No tricks or else."

Carver climbed into the trailer, then pulled the woman up alongside him. The Steel Wheel's light didn't penetrate beyond those first few crates, and the trailer's dank air grew grimier the further they ventured; a dozen paces on the crate wall opened into an empty space. Carver heard the woman's footsteps falter, and in the split-second lull he pivoted, sent a surprise fist into her belly, then fumbled for the electrical switch secreted on the wall.

The thrum of a generator filled the trailer. A row of florescent bulbs flickered on, and once Carver's eyes adjusted he savored the woman's reaction to the makeshift dungeon surrounding them. A work bench stocked with a medieval inquisitor's array of whips, chains, pulleys, straps, clamps, drills, and surgical tools lined one soundproofed wall; meathooks hung from the ceiling. Nearby an obstetric table was bolted to the floor. A table saw and chain-link kennel had been installed in the trailer's farthest end.

In the kennel something moved.

"Welcome to the toy box, bitch," Carver declared. "Enjoy your stay."

He flipped a second switch and a steel partition guillotine-dropped behind them, eliminating any escape. Alarm hijacked the woman's features; she'd doubled-over from Carver's sucker punch, and when he kicked her anew she dropped the knife, fell flat, then lay still.

"Well ain't you a disappointment?" Carver taunted. "Thought there was some serious sass in your ass. Turns out you're just pretty paper doll waitin' to be ripped up."

He hefted an iron collar and set of padlocked chains from the work table. The noise agitated the kennel dweller; they moaned and began banging on the cage's grate.

"Stop fussin' back there," Carver yelled. "You'll get yours soon enough. You both will." He snickered. "Always did fancy doin' sisters."

The blonde peered at the kennel. "Luna…?"

"In the flesh, darlin'." Carver knelt beside the woman. "I like keepin' the strays I take in for a little while. Month, maybe two. 'Til I get the hankerin' for somethin' new. Now that you're here, though, it's time to fetch me a dashboard trophy an' break her down into spare parts. Reckon I'll take me a prize from you, too." He grabbed the silver crescent around the woman's neck. "Had my eye on this all night."

Pandemonium exploded in Carver then. His nerve endings ignited; the trailer drained away into palpable darkness.

Then he was running through a forest, blindly, madly, as fast as his burning legs could take him. Carver's blood pumped, his lungs ached, but he dared not stop.

Something was behind him. Heavy in the brush, gaining every step.

This can't be real, Carver objected. Gotta be a nightmare. Gotta be the drugs.

On a steep, rocky rise Carver spotted his pursuer, chimerical in the moonlight—one instance it was a dog, then a boar, then a bear, then a woman, dark-haired, lithe, muscular, drawing an arrow back from a shining bow.

Carver threw a rock at the archer, hoping to spoil her aim. "The fuck are you?" he shouted. "WHO ARE YOU?"

He turned to scamper over the rise when the arrow struck like a hammer blow to his chest and Carver went spiraling, not to the earth but through it, through space, through time, rewinding, reliving each injury he'd ever inflicted, every slice, every burn, every hit, though now he was on the receiving end, absorbing wound upon wound until his system convulsed.

The sound of rushing blood thickened in Carver's skull, and when he finally blinked the trailer's contours returned. His chest hurt so badly he wanted to scream, but his lips wouldn't move, nothing would move, and he didn't understand why until he glanced down and saw the blonde, her eyes narrow wrathful slits as she drove the switchblade through his breastbone.

"Diana sends her regards," she said, but Carver heard her remotely, as if she were at the far end of a long tunnel. He collapsed backwards then, hemorrhaging his nasty, brutish, short life onto the trailer's dirty floor with every heartbeat.

This ain't right, he thought just before the big blackout. I'm the wolf, damn it. I'm the fuckin' wolf, not h—

# # #

A maelstrom came. Police and paramedics, flashing lights and reporters.

"How'd you know?" everyone asked, as if Selene could tell them, as if they would understand. "How'd you know where your sister was?"

The question shadowed her wherever she went. Even doctors and nurses asked during those anxious days when she rarely left Luna's hospital bedside. Her parents did, too, after they'd flown in that second night, but Selene only gave them the same half-truths she'd fed investigators. Luna is what mattered. Family. Blood. Nothing else.

When Selene had opened the kennel with bolt cutters from Daryll's work bench she'd scarcely recognized the collared figure chained within. Luna's emaciated body was a map of atrocity, lacerations, missing nails, broken bones; one of her eyes was swelled shut, a ball gag plugged her mouth.

"...Selene...?" Luna hoarsely whispered once the muzzle was removed. "How...how..."

How did you know?

"Shhh. You're safe now," Selene said as they embraced. "Let's get you home."

That second night, in her parent's hotel room, Selene had her first solid sleep in weeks. Restful, dreamless slumber— nearly so, anyway.

Selene found herself again in those phantom woods, though now she wasn't running, wasn't hunting. In the dusk a shape appeared at the opposite end of a clearing: the cloaked woman, her eyes bright comets, the reclaimed bow in her hands.

For some while the two watched each other. A cloud eventually drifted over the moon, and once it passed a doe occupied the space where the woman stood. The deer remained at the clearing's edge a quiet minute before bounding between the trees. The urge to follow was strong, but a call from the hospital instead jarred Selene awake.

"Your sister's come through the worst of it," Luna's doctor proudly proclaimed. "It'll take some effort, but a complete recovery's in her future. Right now she's up and alert and is asking for you."

A battalion of television news crews swarmed the hospital entrance when Selene arrived. The story had gone viral: the Torture Truck Killer and the siblings who'd stopped him. The public was fascinated; they wanted answers:

"What are the odds one man inadvertently kidnapped two sisters weeks apart in different states?" one reporter cried.

"How did you know where Luna was?" yelled another

"What can explain it?" shouted a third.

From the hospital's front steps Selene peered above the crowd to the distant desert horizon. The long journey was over. The sun was rising.

She smiled and gently fingered the pendant.

"Divine intervention," Selene replied, and walked up the stairs.

Mother had been dead a month, not that you could convince her of it. Once her mind was set on something, Kevin knew there was no changing it. Mayonnaise in the fridge two years out of date? It's fine if as long as it's never been opened. President impeached? The charges were all made up and Congress is in on it.

He'd forgotten how infuriating – and interminable – conversations with her could be. But now he was constantly reminded of it. His eyes were dark and baggy from the lack of sleep, something his dead mother no longer required.

"No, mama, I don't know why they keep it so hot."

He'd tried returning the phone, but couldn't find the little shop, or even the neighborhood he'd wandered into that fateful day. He'd tried pawning it, but the brand was unrecognizable and worthless. He'd even tried throwing it away, only to later feel his pocket vibrating, the phone securely back inside it.

On a hopeless whim Kevin did a search for the manufacturer. There was no cell manufacturer named Eshu – but he did find a reference to Eshu, a messenger god in the Yoruba religion of Nigeria. He was also a trickster god. Some trick.

"Yes, mama, I know she was there late. Well, in fact, she was going to stay over but I couldn't get off the phone. No, she's not that kind of girl."

Not answering wasn't an option. Though he had successfully ignored it in the store, once he had paid for it he could not let it go past three rings before the phone would simply connect and his mother's voice would be on speaker. He couldn't risk that happening again.

He couldn't sleep. He couldn't maintain a relationship. He'd finally lost his job yesterday for taking too many personal breaks. Now he wandered aimlessly, his eyes downcast, stepping intentionally on every sidewalk crack he could find.

He walked in strange parts of town.

He walked in the rain.

He never did find that odd store again.

SOUTHERN KNIGHTS
FLARE
ARCHIVES VOLUME 1
SOUTHERN KNIGHTS
CAPTAIN THUNDER AND BLUE BOLT
ARCHIVES VOLUME 1
ARISTOCRATIC XTRATERRESTRIAL TIME-TRAVELING THIEVES
LEAGUE OF CHAMPIONS
THE MONSTERS' NEXT DOOR

www.ingramcontent.com/pod-product-compliance
Lightning Source LLC
Chambersburg PA
CBHW071423300726
48976CB00004B/1219